P9-DEE-167

The Dogs of Detroit

DRUE HEINZ LITERATURE PRIZE

THE Dogs
OF Detroit

[stories]

BRAD FELVER

F
FEL
c.l

University of Pittsburgh Press

This book is a work of fiction.
Names, characters, businesses, organizations, places,
events, and incidents are either the product of the author's
imagination or are used fictitiously. This
work is not meant to, nor should it be interpreted to,
portray any specific persons living or dead.

Published by the University of Pittsburgh Press,
Pittsburgh, Pa., 15260

Manufactured in the United States of America

Printed on acid-free paper

10 9 8 7 6 5 4 3 2 1

Cataloging-in-Publication data is available from the
Library of Congress

ISBN 13: 978-0-8229-4542-0

Cover photo: Riccardo Pelati / unsplash
Cover design: Regina Starace

For Susie

Contents

Queen Elizabeth / 1

Throwing Leather / 24

Evolution of the Mule / 37

The Era of Good Feelings / 54

How to Throw a Punch / 71

Unicorn Stew / 76

Stones We Throw / 86

In the Walls / 88

Out of the Bronx / 92

Hide-and-Seek / 104

Country Lepers / 112

Praemonitus, Praemunitus / 131

Patriots / 144

The Dogs of Detroit / 150

Acknowledgments / 167

The Dogs of Detroit

Queen Elizabeth

Many years later, knots of grief cinched intractably within her, Ruth still urged her memory back to their first evening together: drinks at a posh restaurant on the shores of Lake Erie, how Gus offered to pay long before the bartender even noticed them, how he spoke so earnestly of dovetail joints. He wore a flannel shirt and carpenter's jeans with fabric gone thin at the knees. He was wiry as a cornstalk and always would be. That night he spoke of how he wanted to make desks. "Desks!" he said, smiling as if he knew how absurd it sounded. For now he had his union card and worked what jobs came his way.

Ruth was working on her Ph.D. in applied mathematics at Case Western, studying stochastics. She spoke at length about her research, which involved probability theory, random variables, and chaotic systems. Gus listened with genuine interest, and when she finally paused to say, "Does that make sense?" he admitted that he wasn't a graduate student, wasn't a student at all, had in fact never been to a college campus. "I doubt I can even spell stochastic," he said, "but I love listening to you talk about it." The only fancy bit of math he knew was about Euclidean planes requiring three points, and this only because he felt strongly that all desks—all tables of any kind—should have only three legs. Two legs could not balance a load, but four created wobbles. Three created a perfect Euclidean plane.

His knowledge seemed so practical compared to her own—how to fix squeaky floorboards, what made a diesel engine different, why oak leaves fell later in the season than maple leaves. She had never met anyone like him at Case or back home in Boston. He was wholly without pretension, frequently offered remarkable compliments, but quickly grew embarrassed when similar compliments were returned. Even that name of his, Gus, seemed clipped short, as if his mother and father considered extra syllables an extravagance.

When the bartender did finally bring the check, Gus reached for his wallet and realized he didn't have nearly enough money. Who had ever heard of $6 bottles of beer? Cold shame spread over him, and he knew immediately that such a gaff would quash the small, snug world they had built during their evening together. But Ruth thought little of it, pulling out a wad of cash while Gus went quiet like a penitent little Catholic boy, which of course he was. What Ruth never told him—never told anyone—was that it was his mortification over such a trifle, so utterly sincere, that made her love him immediately.

He visited her family before she visited his. Theirs was a three-and-a-half-story house of deep maroon brick and cream trim in Beacon Hill and boasted a view of Boston Common. The sidewalks were of cockeyed brick, framed by cobblestones, and the shrubs were manicured into perfect moons.

They sat on a back veranda and ate eggs Florentine. Gus never did see the kitchen or who had prepared the meal. Her father flinched when they shook hands—just a small twitch, barely perceptible—and only later did Gus realize this was because he was a vascular surgeon of some note, ever afraid of rough calluses and strong grips. Her mother had tight gray hair and picked at her food with a single tine of her fork. Gus felt her eyes that morning as he reached for what was almost certainly the improper cutlery.

After brunch, the men separated from the women in a way that felt mannered and Edwardian. Gus stood next to her father on the front stoop and drank down a glass of coconut rum. They watched dog walkers wander the Common. His eyes cruised around all the sights. He had never been so far east, had never experienced the extravagance of an old city. For a long while they didn't speak, and he felt as if he was being tested. Who could maintain the silence longer? Eventually, her father said, "Desks." He nodded ever so slightly. "Is that a growth industry?" It wasn't entirely clear what the suggestion was. Was he afraid he would have to support them himself if they got married? Embarrassed that his daughter was dating a man who owned more than one hammer? Or was this just the easy contempt that New Englanders reserve for midwesterners?

"They didn't know what to make of you," Ruth said on the drive back to Cleveland.

"Unfortunately, I think they knew exactly what to make of me."

"Well," she said, "that's their problem."

Ruth wanted arguments to resolve things, but Gus just needed them to end as soon as possible.

"Stop apologizing," she would say. "You're allowed to disagree."

"But I'm sorry. I hate this."

"If you want to sit in a booth instead of a table, you have to say so."

"I don't have an opinion. You choose."

"You need to have more opinions."

"About tables and booths?"

So Ruth would always win the fights, which was somehow worse than losing them. He made her feel spoiled, not by anything he did or said but because she was and he wasn't. She had never realized it before then. It made her feel cold, like a bully.

Gus's father lived at the end of a long lane in Medina County. Charming Ohio farm country. Ruth searched the cabinets until she found the hand mixer and started making her special pepper biscuit recipe. She chided his father for eating with a napkin tucked into his shirt but in a way that felt playful, like some ancestral joke that ranged back over the decades.

His mother had been dead long enough that they didn't think to explain what had happened. It was clear enough that they both liked having a woman in the house again.

"A doctorate," his father said, shaking his head. "Must be a lot of work."

"I guess I've always known I would have to do it," Ruth said. She then drank off the last bit of her coffee and stared out the window at the flat green fields.

Later, while Gus hand-washed the dishes, Ruth sat at the table with his father. "That sounds like some house you have there in Boston," he said. They hadn't been speaking of home or her family. It was obvious how close Gus was to his father.

"It's so lovely here," Ruth said. "The quiet, I guess I mean. And there's something about always being able to see the horizon that's comforting."

That afternoon, Gus walked her the length of the property, down long fencerows where he showed her how to scare up rabbits from their dens until she told him to stop being mean. She wanted to pet a chicken but lost her nerve at the last instant. They tried to reach around the ancient bur oak in the barnyard, the largest tree she had ever seen, but even together their arms were swallowed up by its girth. "We call her Queen Elizabeth," he said, explaining that the tree was roughly the same age as Shakespeare. She had always thought New England was old. Such grandeur, she thought, and such different grandeur than what she was accustomed to. How could something be so regal and so unassuming at the same time?

He led her through the outbuildings full of equipment. Where the wood siding met the ground it had mostly shriveled up with rot. Finally he guided her into the workshop, where she quizzed him on what each tool did, and he explained it to her, carefully and without a trace of smugness. The planer and the table saw and the jointer—they had all been his grandfather's, had been made in Germany. Nothing even approached their quality anymore. She pulled open drawers and fingered drill bits and awls and rasps. "There's a tool for everything," he told her, "and most of them are good for only one very specific thing."

"This will all be yours one day," she said, and he said, "Not soon, I hope."

In the middle of the floor sat a magnificent desk, wood still raw and unstained. Clean lines, trim like Gus himself. Not a trace of excess flourish to be seen. Solid, squared legs, tapered to a slender tip. Three legs only, always three legs, he said, again referencing the perfection of a Euclidean plane. Old-growth walnut, he went on, taking her hand and tracing it over the grain pattern, all harvested locally. He pointed out the dovetails in the lap drawer, the through-mortises on the legs. She felt she understood him better then, the artist lurking underneath those flannel shirts of his.

"It's for your father," he told her.

They had each other there on the desk. He was slow and deliberate, polite even in lovemaking, his callused hand never leaving the curve of her neck. It smelled of sawdust, and for the rest of her life, when she smelled that smell, flickers of arousal would warm her from the inside out.

A growing swell of energy between them, they each felt it, the way it lashed them together. Slowly they wormed themselves into each other's lives, not always the grandest moments—holidays or great traumas—but the smaller, daily gestures: kissing with bad breath, boiling hot dogs for dinner, changing flat tires in the brutal Cleveland winter.

They talked about how happy they were as if afraid that they must decipher it daily, how astonishing it all was, or risk it diluting right in front of them.

"I don't want to take your name," Ruth said. "I've had this name all my life and I'm used to it now."

"You don't have to."

"But what about our kids? It'll be too confusing."

"Your mother wouldn't understand," he said.

"Yes," she said. "Her." She looked out the window, squinting into the sun. "We both know I won't hyphenate."

"We could make a new name. Both of us."

"Something fun?"

"Something tough."

They each wrote down their choices. She chose *Ivers*. He chose *Bazooka*.

In the end, she took his name because they didn't want to spend the rest of their lives explaining it at dinner parties.

Ruth miscarried deep into her second trimester. A problem with the umbilical cord. For a week they stayed in their little apartment, curtains drawn, the air thick like after rain. Sometimes she wanted to be close to him, nuzzling into his chest, and other times she just needed him not to look at her. These waves came suddenly, and he learned how to recognize them. He didn't understand them, but he knew it wasn't important that he did.

"I'm okay," she insisted, "but I just can't stop picturing the cord like a noose around his little neck." For a long while she went back to the diaphragm without telling Gus. She was terrified of her own body and didn't want him to know. Sex changed from something they did together into something that was done *to* her.

They spent weekends with his father on the farm and never told her parents at all. She took the rest of the semester off, technically to finish her dissertation, though she accomplished little. They adopted a dog, which generally brought more agony than joy. When it pooped on the carpet, Gus chased it around with a drywall hammer; when it ran away he stapled signs to telephone poles. He had wanted an Irish Setter, but Ruth wanted a Pomeranian. He joked with friends that they compromised by getting a Pomeranian.

A few months later they went out to dinner and drank too

much wine. She laughed like a teenager and sat cross-legged in her chair. They tossed bits of uncooked macaroni into each other's glasses and then apologized to their waiter. When dessert came she got quiet again as if some shadow had descended. She stared into her glass and picked at the polish on her forefinger. "I'm so, so sorry," she said, and he knew then they would haul this on their backs for the rest of their lives.

Her father died in March, and his father died in June. They both realized then that the last traces of childhood were gone. She thought the wakes would be dramatically different, but they weren't, hushed voices and hollow platitudes for rich people and poor people alike. She wasn't terribly sad but had to pretend she was; he was devastated but had to act like he wasn't. And so for several months it seemed as if they weren't talking to each other so much as to the emissaries they sent out into the world.

One night she found him sitting on the toilet lid. The door was closed and the light was off, but she knew he was in there. "What are you doing?" she asked.

"I don't know," he said. "I guess I'm trying."

She sat on the floor in front of him. The Pomeranian stood in the doorway, guarding them, like it knew things weren't right.

"He told me once that your desks were his favorite things." His father had never really said that to her, but she inferred a great deal from his long proud looks.

They writhed together there on the cold tile floor. He was manic, desperate, even a bit rough with her, which he never was before or after.

They named her Annabelle. They had never been so exhausted or so happy. Gus could scarcely bring himself to take on jobs that stole him away. Ruth officially abandoned her dissertation, all those years of work that suddenly seemed frivolous.

Gus built Annabelle a crib of cherry, with lovely tapered spindles and long finger joints. He was afraid of SIDS—it was all you ever saw on the local news—and so he often slept in the chair next to the crib. He strummed a toy ukulele for her. It wasn't long before Annabelle learned how to smile. D minor and G were her favorite chords, and for hours he would play them, the D minor hovering like a Frisbee in flight, just out of reach, until he would finally resolve it with the G, and little Annabelle would smile and kick.

One evening when Gus was working late, Ruth was alone with Annabelle. They hadn't eaten yet, and she was trying to apply for jobs. Their budget had become frighteningly thin. She stirred a pot on the stove and held Annabelle and scrolled through a list of academic positions, then secretarial ones. It was all too much. She wanted to scream and chuck rocks through the windows. Here she was: a mother, but was she anything else? Anything at all? Mother-hood had seized her destiny while she had been too busy to notice. Fathers were somehow exempt from this fate. She hated Gus for being gone, hated herself for quitting her dissertation, hated Ohio most of all. Then Annabelle threw up on her shoulder, and before Ruth could clean it up or set her down, her daughter had started gumming up the vomit.

She told Gus about it when he got home.

"She ate her own puke?"

"Sorry. Jesus."

"What color was the puke?"

"I don't know. Purple maybe? I think we had plums earlier." Gus held Annabelle up and looked at her. "Hi, there, my little puke-eater. Next time we could cook it for you first. That seems like our job. Your mother can do wonders with garlic and a little olive oil. You could have yourself a nice puke fritter!"

He gave her a bath and read her one book after another before bed. Ruth listened from outside the bedroom door as Gus made his outlandish voices and Annabelle giggled. It often worked this way: all day she fought off a manic craving for a break, only to find that when it finally came, there was little joy in it. By the time she got back to her job applications, the toyish strums of the ukulele pulsed out from the bedroom, washing over her like a sleeping serum.

Gus would sometimes lay playful traps for her, which made her feel young and loved:

"If you had to change one thing about me, what would it be?" he asked.

"That's not fair."

"That's the point."

She thought for a moment. "I'd make you twenty pounds heavier."

"I'm serious."

"I am too," she said. "It would make me feel thinner. I gain weight like a normal person but you just keep on looking like some teenage bronco rider."

Years later, when she emptied the trash bin in his workshop, she found dozens of empty Archway cookie packages. At first she was terribly confused—he had virtually no sweet tooth to speak of—and only after some thought did she remember.

Annabelle started preschool, and suddenly every wall in the house grew crowded with crayon artwork. Their friends became the parents of Annabelle's classmates, their free time split between swimming lessons and playgrounds and the zoo. Ruth took a position as an office manager for a pet food distributor. Gus began selling a few more desks, working late rehabbing grand staircases in Cleveland Heights and Willoughby and Hudson. They bought an old Craftsman home with pipes that knocked when they flushed toilets. They put rugs over the old oak floors and let Annabelle chase them from room to room while she screamed like a Viking. Blanket forts dominated their living room for weeks at a time. They raked leaves and jumped in the piles. They became experts about dinosaurs and then sea shells and then paper airplane design.

Without noticing it, they had created an entire country with its own language and customs and mythologies and even defensive perimeters. Their own lines allowed few breaches. Their country was complete on its own. A wide world existed beyond their borders, they could still hear its bustling chaos, but they were content to ignore it and to be ignored in kind.

The doctors found the tumor in Annabelle's brain when she was four years old. It was the size of a robin's egg, malignant, and needed to come out.

"But you can do surgery, can't you?" Ruth asked.

"We're not sure yet," the doctor said. That phrase—*We're not sure yet*—became an oft-heard refrain through months of consultations, and they learned it had a very specific meaning: *We are quite sure, and it's bad news.*

They saw specialists in a dozen cities: Pittsburgh, Orlando, Denver, Los Angeles, Toronto. Ruth was ferocious in her research, in her preparation for each appointment, bringing with her pages of questions that she asked like accusations. The numbers gave her something to focus on, though quantifying bad luck in such a way also made her want to murder the universe.

"Do you know the odds of this happening?" Ruth asked one time. "Sixty-eight million to one," she said. "Sixty-eight million."

Gus looked down at her legal pad, the scratches and strange symbols, Greek or Latin, perhaps. He sometimes forgot about her imposing mathematical pedigree, which now became a prison, intellect stunting emotion. What was the point of calculating probabilities or the effects of random elements? Gus wanted to know. They were here already. These calculations served only to make him feel like a helpless victim. What he didn't understand, of course, was that they allowed Ruth a respite, precious moments of cold, abstract thought. Through them, she could quarantine her despair so that it would not pollute everyone around her.

They drove to Boston to see a specialist her father had known at Mass General. She was from Mumbai and had a long name that Gus could not pronounce. The doctor paged through Annabelle's chart, frowning and shaking her head without speaking. When she finally looked up, she smiled at them, but it was the kind of smile offered to a dear friend at a funeral.

"No more bad news," Ruth said.

This specialist was aiming to lead a trial of an experimental treatment that involved first inducing a coma and then utilizing a special cocktail of drugs that would, perhaps, target the ravenous tumor.

"She's a good candidate, isn't she?" Ruth asked, not completely a question.

The doctor leaned in with a bowl of candy and told Annabelle to take as much as she could hold. Ruth realized then that this doctor had done this many times, was as expert in delivering bad news as she was in the operating room.

"I won't presume to understand what you are going through," she said. She spoke with that peculiar British Indian accent, which Ruth decided meant she had likely been educated at Cambridge or Oxford. "My father was a particle physicist and my mother died when I was a teenager. He could be a harsh man, largely devoid of human sentiment. He forbade me grieving over my mother's death because he believed there was no reason, scientifically speaking, to do so. According to the law of conservation of mass, she was still with us. Mass cannot be created or destroyed, of course. In fact, he pointed out, the very atoms from my mother's body were now repurposed in our own bodies. This is true of every human who has ever lived. Every human currently alive is composed of the very atoms of every person who has ever lived. Every person! Billions of atoms from each person. Can you imagine? A billion atoms that make me a person once made Shakespeare a person, and Cleopatra and Gandhi and Einstein."

"Also Hitler and Stalin," Ruth said. "Genghis Khan, Oliver Cromwell, Caligula, Attila, Jeffrey Dahmer."

"Ruth."

The doctor ignored this and handed Annabelle another sucker.

"So, scientifically speaking," Ruth said, "we cannot be sad."

"Ruth," Gus said, more pleading than scolding.

"Well," the doctor said but then said nothing else.

Gus insisted on making the casket himself, long hours alone in the workshop, and he was unable to see the strange selfishness of this. It was a refuge he refused to share with her. He fixated most on the casket dimensions, hardly larger than a laundry basket.

"Why are you punishing yourself like this?" Ruth asked.

"She'll be in there forever."

"Come home," she said, but he had already gone back to work.

They couldn't even hold hands at the funeral or feign unity at the wake. They each faced the same choice at this moment—anger or sadness—and each opted for anger. Perhaps this was not a conscious decision. The world had drained them of compassion until no residue remained. Anger seemed easier, cleaner, almost tangible. But in the coming years, each of them would look back at this time, searching for the precise moment they pivoted away from each other, because if they could isolate the fulcrum, the singularity, perhaps some wormhole would sprout and revive a conduit to the past.

Ruth said awful things and then felt horrible about them, but then she would say more awful things. It was an addiction she could not kick, as if discarding her grief and forcing him to bear it instead. *You can't play ukulele and fix this, you know. You always wanted a boy anyway. She'll never need one of your desks now.*

If Ruth said awful things, Gus said nothing at all. He retreated to the farm, to the workshop, where he could easily make her feel like an interloper. He spent whole days there, while Ruth sat at home, waiting for him to return to her, though he never truly did. She began to spend weekends in Boston. For months they lingered on this way, trapped in a stalemate.

Ruth appeared at the workshop one afternoon. Gus had been mindlessly sanding the tapered legs of a desk for several hours, his arm ached from it, and as he stood to look at his work, he realized he had sanded so much that the third leg was now noticeably thinner than its counterparts.

Ruth sighed. "I need a break."

"Me too," he said.

"From you. From all of this. I don't expect you to understand."

Gus dropped the sanding block, and it rattled on the concrete floor.

"Do you have to act like this?"

"How am I acting?"

"Like the spoiled little rich girl."

He'd never once spoken to her that way. Halfway through saying it he already felt horrible. He didn't love her any less now, but everything around them had changed, as if they were standing still while a storm swept through around them.

Ruth sat down on the cold concrete and suddenly looked very young and very fragile. For a moment Gus had some hope, the smallest breach. But her face was drawn, had grown tighter, menacing.

"We can use a lawyer we know," she said. "Charlie's brother, I guess. Keep it all simple."

"Simple," he said.

It was stunning how quickly their country could crumble. Civil war. A dozen years to construct but only a few months to collapse.

Gus started moving his things out of the house the next week. At first Ruth was still there, but by the time he was nearly finished, she managed to be absent. The last hours he moved slowly, one small box at a time, adding in extra, unnecessary trips. What did he hope for? A change of heart at the last minute? A dramatic reconciliation where they fell to the wet ground and kissed?

He found a note on the kitchen counter, just a small Post-it, as if Ruth did not even care if Gus found it: *It's different for mothers.*

He stared at the letter. It demanded that he develop a fresh emotional response, one that hadn't yet been charted and classified by scientists: profoundly sad and confused and resentful and sad again around the edges. Such hardness in her. Jesus, he thought, halfway wishing he were capable of such hardness also. How easily grief could mutate into something else entirely. She was right, of course: there were things that only mothers were capable of, like lifting cars off their children during tornadoes. Like this.

He left the note where it was. He needed her to wonder for the rest of her life if he even saw it. Initially, he had planned on leaving her the Pomeranian, but the note stopped him. He made room in the front seat, where it curled into a ball and fell asleep as they drove away.

Gus moved back to the farm. He leased the land: soy, wheat, corn, hay. Days he worked jobs in Cleveland—elaborate built-ins, mantels, newel posts hickory spindles on wide staircases—and evenings he built desks, the glow of the old workshop spilling into the barnyard late into the night. He ate microwave dinners in his underwear and left the telephone off the hook. He became a ghost, the sort of man that people in a small town recognize, though no one can recall ever speaking to.

Ruth sold the house to the first offer. She couldn't be in Ohio any longer. She moved back to Boston, where her mother still lived, and soon she was attending fundraisers and charity auctions in the ballrooms of the most elegant old hotels. She found herself surrounded by people so wealthy they had no need to locate Ohio on a map. The city offered as many distractions as she needed, faces new to her and those whom she had known many years earlier when they were thinner and more eager.

Ruth eventually settled in with a man named Harold Gutman. He had worked as an intern under her father and kept a trimmed beard, mostly gray now, and had a single bumper sticker on his BMW, which read, very simply, "DOCTOR." Ruth found this a strange and gaudy touch for a man who otherwise largely passed through the world undetected. When he started speaking of marriage, she would turn away and tell him that she wasn't so sure, not yet. She still had so many things to sort out, tangled linkages in her brain. It was in the evenings when Harold Gutman would invariably make such hints, always after a few drinks. He never proposed outright, only took her temperature, which was icy for many years, though he was convinced a thaw would eventually come.

"I'm just not *sure*," Ruth would always say if he pressed her. Of course, she was perfectly sure, perfectly sure she did not want to marry Harold Gutman, did not want to marry again, ever.

It was this incessant talk of marriage which pushed her back into her dissertation. She needed something to occupy her evenings in order avoid Harold Gutman's affections, and so she holed herself up in the wood-paneled study, finally finishing eight years after Annabelle's death. She declined to walk at the commencement ceremony because she did not want to travel back to Cleveland. Instead, she strolled the Back Bay streets alone, and when she returned to their apartment, she found on her desk a sticker of the letter S, which Harold Gutman had left for her. Together they would be "DOCTORS" for all the world to see.

When the Pomeranian died, Gus buried it behind the barn. He stood in front of the old rotary wall phone, ready to dial Ruth and deliver the news. It was all he could think to do. Should he or not? They hadn't spoken in years. He wouldn't even know how to say hello. Old lovers were far worse than strangers. Should he use her name or not?

Hello, Ruth.
Ruth, hello, it's Gus.
Hi, there, it's me.
Ruthie, dear, I'm sorry to deliver such bad news.

When he finally dialed, a man's voice answered, and he hung up immediately.

Ruth took an adjunct position at a local community college, teaching a course or two each semester. It felt like a concession, but she ended up liking her students, most of whom were bright and engaged. Some days she would stay on campus for eight or ten hours, teaching and meeting with students. She loved most how they would stomp into her office, breathless and full of absurd excuses. She would come home and tell Harold Gutman about them. "Even when they say ridiculous things, they're so enthusiastic about it," she said.

"What about children then?" Harold Gutman asked her one evening after a benefit at the Park Plaza. He'd allowed himself an extra glass of wine and was feeling warm and confident.

She squinted, though it was dark in their bedroom. "We're too old for that, Harold." She was only forty-six but felt much older.

"We could adopt."

"It's nice of you to say that, but no, we couldn't."

Harold Gutman didn't pursue it after that. No marriage, no family of their own. Instead, her students would become her children, in a way that was common but not terribly healthy.

When a full-time teaching post opened up, Ruth took it. "If your father were still alive" was all her mother would say to the news, which was the harshest sort of admonishment she could muster at the thought of a community college. Harold Gutman too seemed perplexed. "Isn't it terribly repetitive?" he asked, and she told him that of course it was. "I don't like surprises or changes the way I used to."

At a conference in Phoenix, she slept with a young assistant professor of statistics. He was barely thirty and played video games on his cell phone. He was aggressive in bed like an upperclassman in a fraternity. In the morning, when she woke and saw him there splayed atop the covers, naked and hairy, she immediately thought of what a horrible thing she had just done to Gus. How would she admit this to him? Would he ever forgive her? It was only at breakfast, when they sat in relative silence, that she realized she meant Harold Gutman. It was Harold Gutman whom she had betrayed.

Several years later Ruth took a stroll down Newbury Street, not so much interested in buying anything as in walking the promenade the way people do after a harsh winter. She was just about to turn back for home when she saw in the front window of a store a three-legged desk. That unmistakable aesthetic: austere, unassuming, clean.

"It's a gorgeous piece, isn't it?" the salesman said. He wore a tailored vest, no tie, buttons undone through the hollow of his chest.

"It's beautiful."

"A relatively new artist, just breaking onto the scene in the last few years. He lives in Iowa, I believe—Iowa or Ohio—and crafts everything individually, which is unheard of anymore."

"It's beautiful," she said again.

"This desk is made from bur oak and features through-mortises and a tripod—all of his desks do." He eased out the lap drawer. "He does all the dovetails by hand, no jig. You can see the Shaker and Pennsylvania Dutch influences, of course, but he has carved out new territory. Remarkable work, lines as distinct as I've seen since Tom Moser."

Ruth traced her fingers across the edges of the desktop. She could smell the workshop, the arousal taking shape in her. Sparks that had hidden themselves away, dormant for many years.

"We're thrilled to have some of his pieces here," the salesman said. He was young and very fashionable and seemed afraid of Ruth's silence. "Ordinarily our New York and London stores get first crack, but they've done remarkably well here. All the young students, perhaps. People want smaller, cleaner desks now. Computers are smaller than ever. No more of those shelved, multilevel monstrosities of the eighties and nineties. That's the trend, anyway." He slid the lap drawer back in. "Quite the visionary."

The pain from this encounter was real, and yet so was the excitement. Ruth was alternately sad and angry, though she couldn't deny she felt more alive than she had in many years. She became convinced Gus's aim was to torture her. He could have sold desks anywhere. Why Boston? Why so close to her parents' old brownstone? Clearly, he wanted to force a confrontation between them where he would reveal to her . . . what? His children, his beautiful new wife? How he had survived and moved on? He would not say a word, but he would parade them in front of her. That was very like him, the quietest possible revenge.

But then other days she thought that perhaps Gus simply wanted to see her and didn't know how. He would kiss her on the cheek, tell her how he had missed her, how differently his life had ended up without her. And then he would look down and say, "Could we just talk about her now?" And she would cry, and he would cry, and they would talk about her all night.

She found herself distracted during her lectures, and more than once she had to excuse herself into the hallway. For months this happened at regular—and then increasing—intervals. Harold Gutman noticed the change in her, but she told him it was just the stress of teaching.

Gus had burrowed his way back into that small nook of her brain where the trauma still lingered, quiet for many years but never truly dormant. His appearance had disturbed a system at rest, jolting it back into a slow but accelerating orbit that would slowly consume her. But Ruth surrendered to this freely, as if leaning into a strong wind, considering for the first time in many years that perhaps memory can exist without despair.

Harold Gutman didn't understand why he needed a new desk. His old one worked perfectly well, and besides, he was used to it.

"This one is just better," Ruth said.

"I liked all the drawers and nooks in my old one. Where will I put everything now?"

"You'll get rid of things. That's the point."

He frowned, unconvinced. She sauntered over to the desk, leaned against its edge, and slid off her heels. She unbuttoned her blouse and leaned back, trying to appear seductive but feeling ridiculous.

"What are you doing?" Harold Gutman asked.

"I'm showing you how much better this desk is."

"But we have a bed, a big comfortable bed. And I don't think it can support us both. It seems to be missing one leg."

She bought more desks, at first just to furnish guest bedrooms, then two more for the house Harold Gutman kept on the Cape, then more that she put directly into a storage bay. Eventually, the young furniture salesman asked what she'd been hoping he'd ask. "I'd be happy to arrange an introduction," he said, "for such a generous fan of his work. He's in town occasionally."

"Oh, I don't know," Ruth said, suddenly feeling diffident as a teenager.

"I haven't met him myself, but he's supposed to be a modest, quiet sort of man. With all his success, he supposedly still lives in an old farmhouse in the middle of Iowa."

She told him it wasn't at all necessary, there was no need to go to such trouble. She just adored his desks was all. The salesman shrugged, unconcerned. Later that night, though, she dialed the number on his business card and told him that she had changed her mind. She would like to meet the artist the next time he came to Boston.

It was a Saturday in October when she arrived at the store to see him. She told Harold Gutman she had an appointment with a student, and he nodded, suspecting a lie was hidden somewhere. He had noticed her fussing in the mirror far longer than usual. They both knew they were clinging to the threads of whatever they had, like the last day of a vacation that is spent mostly on travel.

Wet leaves painted the sidewalks on Newbury Street. When she entered the store, Gus's back was to her, but he was the same as ever. Hadn't gained a single pound, though he'd gone fully gray. He wore carpenter's jeans and a flannel shirt. As she drew nearer she realized that the pants weren't just of a style; they were the exact pair he often wore years earlier. She recognized a stain above the left pocket.

How long had it been? She'd become horrible with dates. Twenty years? That sounded about right.

"Jesus," he said when he turned around. It took him several moments before he could compose himself. Ruth felt absurd. She had hoped that he knew, that he had actively targeted Boston, but Gus seemed truly shocked.

They strolled down Newbury Street. Gus clasped his hands behind his back and took long, loping strides. He glanced over at her and smiled that calm smile she remembered. Strangers often took this for arrogance, but she knew it was just his quiet nature. *Silence is something that should be protected*, his father used to say.

"How's the farm?" she asked.

"The same." He stopped walking and looked up at the roofs of the buildings, tarnished copper and clay tile. He frowned. "That's not true. I don't know why I just said that. Queen Elizabeth died," he said. "Came down in a bad storm a few years ago."

"No!" she said.

He nodded. "More than a few years ago now, I guess. I built a kiln next to the barn and cured all the lumber I could, some thousands of board-feet."

"And the desks?"

He nodded. "Bur oak is just about all I've worked with ever since."

"I could tell you still use the handsaw for the dovetails. You always did hate those jigs."

"You do something one certain way for long enough, and you become incapable of doing it any other way." It was just like him to say something like that. But it made her feel more like a client than the mother of his dead daughter.

He stepped off the curb to allow a mother with a stroller to pass. Ruth watched the woman and child move away from them, then disappear around the corner.

"I suppose Queen Elizabeth is still in our bodies, isn't she? Or her atoms anyway."

Gus looked at her quizzically for a moment, and then he remembered. He nodded but said nothing.

They walked on in silence for several minutes, and then Ruth said, "I hated that doctor. But her story stuck with me. I guess that's obvious, isn't it? When I went back to my research after all those years, I tried to calculate it. How many atoms from the dead might migrate to the living. It became this strange obsession, not at all related to my dissertation. It took a long time, but I eventually worked out a reasonable prediction and asked a scientist on campus about it, and he pointed out that my math was generally good, but I'd overlooked one basic error of physics."

"That it takes far too long," Gus said. "Centuries for them to dissipate."

"You, too?" Ruth asked, and Gus touched her arm, telling her yes. She froze, his hand warm on her skin, afraid that the smallest movement might dislodge them.

After a few moments, they noticed they were blocking the sidewalk and had to move on. "So, Queen Elizabeth isn't actually in us," Ruth said and paused. "Never will be."

"No," Gus said, "but she'll end up in someone eventually."

They started walking again. He dug his hands into his pockets and gazed around. She felt a sadness in him that had never been there. A hollow look in his eyes. Whether it was all the talk of death or long-term loneliness or just the general cruelties of life, she couldn't know. The truth was they had been apart far longer than they'd been together. Could she even claim to know him anymore?

They ended up at an outdoor cafe, drinking tea. Ruth warmed her hands on her mug and sipped slowly. Gus noticed that the table wobbled on the uneven bricks, and so he shimmed one leg with a folded napkin. They both felt uneasy, wishing they'd gone to a bar instead, where it becomes easier for old lovers to ignore how well they know each other's bodies.

"I can't believe no one else snatched you up," she said.

"Well," he said, "I doubt I made it very easy." He looked away, his eyes training to all the commotion on the street. "When Queen Elizabeth died, it was strange at first not having a tree there, like a pulled tooth when all you can do is trace the gap with your tongue." He set his tea down. "Then I found myself sweating all the time. It took me over a year to realize that the house itself retained that much more heat with the tree gone. No more shade." He paused and for a moment seemed ready to weep, but then he coughed and looked away.

"I know what you mean," Ruth said. "It felt so strange when I moved back to Boston, like I didn't actually grow up here." She didn't tell him how for years she would think about him in the middle of the day, how some silly little thing would happen and she would make a mental note to tell him when she got home, only to remember hours later that she couldn't.

They went back to their tea, their own thoughts. It hurt Ruth to see the many ways Gus was still the same man, how her absence had not changed that, but it also hurt to see the many ways he was now different, to know that she'd had no hand in shaping his new quirks. He still palmed his mug rather than using the handle, but he took smaller sips now, probably because he moved slower. He was older, but he was also successful, could accomplish fewer things each day. He probably appreciated success in ways that she never would.

"It's strange seeing me, isn't it?" she asked. "I can tell it's strange for you."

He squinted at her for a long time, and she began to worry that he would never respond. She was thinking of that terrible note she had left him, though she wasn't certain if he'd even seen it. Finally, he said, "Not strange, no." But then he stopped talking and grimaced. "It's like having phantom limb syndrome. I feel you over there, and I know you belong over here, but you're there and I'm here and there's no changing that."

A warmth crept into her limbs, like muscles being stretched. She had forgotten how his words could puncture straight through to her core. All these years separated hadn't changed him in the important ways. She cried then. It was a dirty, messy sort of cry, not at all dignified. All the grief of her life seemed to surface: a loveless mother and father, an unfulfilling career, dead children, dead relationships. She couldn't look at Gus. He didn't reach for her or offer a tissue, just let her have it out as privately as possible.

"I just worked," he said, hoping to give her more time to recover herself. "Eventually, I could go five minutes without thinking about her, and that was a revelation. I learned how to function without pressuring myself to find joy in anything. But five minutes is as long as I ever got. Never more than that, not even now."

She already knew that Gus was the only one she could ever talk to about Annabelle, but she realized then it wasn't that simple. It was all they would ever be capable of talking about. But she also realized that it was the only thing she wanted to talk about, and that would be true for the rest of her life.

When she'd composed herself, she said, "It's hard to know that you've used up all the good parts of your life so early."

She wanted him to disagree but he nodded. "Thank God we're still young," he said, perhaps as a joke, but perhaps not.

They didn't speak for several minutes after that, and neither of them had any intention to. It was the silence of age, if not of wisdom, and also the silence of those who have weathered the worst long before and now have little fear of the world's residual cruelties. Occasionally their eyes met and lingered, but they managed only to grin at each other as if they shared some private secret that they would never try to articulate, not even to each other. Eventually, the waiter approached and silently placed the check between them—perhaps he saw that neither of them wore a wedding ring and wanted to be proper—and there it would stay, each of them ignoring it, hoping they might sit together just a few moments longer.

Throwing Leather

We were mean kids. We knew it and we celebrated it. We salted slugs in the street and watched them melt. We caught brook trout and plucked out their eyes with a corkscrew, leaving their wriggling bodies for the bears. We slathered each other's sandwiches with gear grease when no one was looking. When we got hurt or punished, we took it as a sign that we were doing something right, that we were being mean enough. But Charley was always searching for new cruelties. Even his mother was afraid of him, which meant he mostly did as he pleased.

Charley was an angry kid, not overly large but ferocious. He had no interest in anyone our age or their television and video games. When he bothered to go to school at all everyone shied away from him because he smelled like diesel fuel or gunpowder or carcass. He sneered at teachers. He inspired awe even from the most seasoned kids because he would disappear for days at a time, trudging through the unkempt cemetery that bordered our backyard and into the dense woods, and just when rumors started to circulate that he was gone for good, he emerged with crusted blood on his arms and face and never bothered to tell anyone where he'd been or how he killed whatever he killed.

This was Cut Bank, northern Montana, grizzly country, where goofy tourists wore bells on their belts and carried bear spray that claimed to be napalm in a can and was sold at every corner gas station. It was a fine product if you encountered a black bear, but they were basically pets anyway. Trailhead signs even advised hikers to punch them right in the nose, and they would run away, which they did. Grizzlies, though, were part dinosaur, remnants of an earth where animals the size of Volkswagens stomped around and ate goddamned whatever they wanted. Your only hope with a grizzly, the saying went, was to punch its stomach walls enough that it might digest you faster. Even the traps poachers left in the hills looked like medieval torture devices, enough rusted toothy steel to keep a Gulf Stream tethered to the ground. Every couple years, it seemed some determined suburbanite wandered into the wild looking to prove something to his kids or wife or mistress. Within a few days, Charley and I would see the vultures circling high above his heading, swooping around in their cockeyed figure-eight formation, and then a couple days later, we'd read in the newspaper what we already knew.

Cut Bank was a raw world, a place that progress had ignored, and we were fine with it. Everyone was a bit crude, like we had first wandered out of the wilderness only weeks earlier—the men always unshaven and frowning, the women with tangled, knotty hair. A place like Missoula might have been New York City to us. Only our proximity to the national park forty miles west was proof to the tourists that we could behave like civilized folk.

Charley wandered the hills and the streets of Cut Bank with what had been his father's Winchester .444 and had no fear of grizzlies or tourists or anyone except my father. Even when he stayed with us in civilization, he liked to invent violent games with strict parameters that tested your manliness. "New game," he would always say, and then we would practice it, fine-tuning the rules to eliminate the nudge—the pussy, the chicken liver, the weakling—which was the worst thing a human could be.

Years earlier, my mother and Charley's father died in a car accident that left many questions unanswered. (His trousers had been at his knees, and she hadn't been wearing her seatbelt.) We became a sort of leftover family. Charley and his mother moved into our squat concrete house, which had only two bedrooms. My father never claimed it was something other than the obvious. They shared a room and a bed, and Charley and I did the same, and I suppose this was some kind of misguided justice. Starla, Charley's mother, was a thin, doe-eyed woman who smoked more than she ate and managed to over-boil a hot dog. When she did speak, it was so quiet that you learned to just nod at things you couldn't quite hear.

Charley ignored her so casually it seemed Starla could have been his pestering younger sister. She asked little of him—to go to school at least twice a week, not to leave his loaded rifle on the counter, not to talk about her dead husband at dinner—but Charley couldn't do it. He chose not to. But when he disobeyed long enough or called her something too ugly, my father would step in, telling Charley to apologize or get thumped, and Charley always sneered his sorries and wandered off somewhere. My father took Charley on as an accessory to having Starla move in. Charley dealt with my father because he couldn't sleep outside during a Cut Bank winter.

"The first one to complain about your mother's cooking," my father said early on, "becomes the new chef." He pointed to Starla when he said "mother" but spoke to us both. "I don't enjoy thumping you boys, but you know I will," he added. Starla looked at the ground as if embarrassed that someone would take so much time to defend her. So we never complained.

"New game," Charley said when we avoided the house. Then we stole bikes from outside the convenience store, tucked push-brooms under our arms, and jousted each other down the middle of the street. First one to get knocked off had to eat a pinecone. First one to complain about soreness in the ribs lost use of his chariot for the next round and had to run down the spray-painted joust lane. First one to bleed was a nudge.

When we tired of bike jousting, we took up cat hunting. I used a pry bar; Charley used a hatchet. Whoever brought home the most cat tails won. No time limit. If you tried to pass off roadkill and got caught, you had to eat it. If you came home empty-handed, you were a nudge.

The first time we played, I killed three—all mangy, hopeless-looking things—and came home at dark. Charley stayed out all night. He shook me awake before sunrise with eleven cat tails dangling from his belt loops.

When my father found the cat tails under our bed, he thumped us. At first, Charley stood with him, tried to make an honest showing of it, but my father was a large man, a real bruiser, and Charley ended up with a fat, red face. "Wherever the bodies are, boys," my father said, "go find them. You kill it, you eat it." So, we trudged back out, both on the same team, to find our cats. We skinned and gutted them, then tossed their bones and guts into a shallow pit in the cemetery. We roasted the rest until they tasted like charcoal, both to burn the rot out of them and because neither of us wanted to know what cat tasted like. Charley cursed my father under his breath, but he also ate his share.

We hid our cat tails better after that.

At night, when we couldn't compete, we closed our bedroom door and pretended, smoked Winstons and set up hypothetical scenarios to root out the nudge. That we had to disagree for the game to work was understood.

You're in a cage with another man. Do you want a .22 with only one round or dull pirate sword?

You're interrogating a terrorist. Do you want a scalpel or a jar full of lava?

The neighbor's dog keeps barking all night. Do you kill the dog or the neighbor?

What wild animal would Starla be? On this alone we agreed: pigeon.

Then my father brought home a set of boxing gloves and taught us to throw the leather. He could only afford one set, so one hand threw the leather and the other hand threw the flesh, which hurt a lot more. At first we just attacked each other like wild dogs, but we soon learned that you couldn't keep up that sort of pace for more than a minute or so. Those fights ended early, before there was a clear winner and a clear nudge, and so we had to learn a more measured approach.

It was humiliating at first. Nothing natural about throwing a punch. Range of motion is too loose, too many options that beg to be combined and leave you wide open. You have to commit to one, be precise. Speed and precision over power, always.

The second week Charley caught me high on the neck, right on my Adam's apple. "Christ, Jack," he said when I sat on the ground sucking air in between rounds, "your neck's the size of a watermelon."

I hadn't felt anything before that. There's no pain during a fight. That usually surfaces in the morning. Charley ran inside and took Starla's makeup mirror and showed me. It was already red and bulging, and when I opened my mouth to talk, the Adam's apple bobbed around as if loose from its hinges.

When I told my father I couldn't eat dinner that night, he thought I was getting smart with him. "We had the talk about your mother's food," he said. "Sit."

But then he saw my neck, laughed and told me to sit still, someone had plucked my apple and that it wasn't all that uncommon for fighters. He looked over at Charley, smirked.

He felt around the swelling, and I gripped the table ledge until the blood drained from my hands, and then all of a sudden he jostled it in a quick movement, and I felt a click like a kneecap sliding back into place. "There," my father said and turned back to his chicken.

In a couple days, the swelling eased, and we went back to tossing punches as hard as we could and gassing before we bloodied each other. My father stood watching us, shaking his head. The injury had piqued his interest. We knew he'd boxed in the marines, and that earned him some respect. "Keep your chin down and elbows tight," he said and demonstrated. "Pivot at the hips. Bend your lead knee. Twist into him to dodge. Don't lean back or you're wide open, and if the other guy knows what's what, he'll pancake you."

Our hands turned rough, leathery, and our exposed knuckles bulged like old tree roots and dislocated often enough that it stopped hurting. We snapped jabs and didn't pull punches, not ever. Charley's nose pudged flat from my straight right, but he didn't mind once my father told him he looked like Primo Carnera. After this, he led more with his face, daring me to pancake him, which I did.

I was better, but Charley was tougher. I was a full head taller and still growing. But Charley was short and skinny and hadn't grown an inch since he was fourteen and never would. Still, even his measured attacks were ferocious. His eyes yellowed as if infected with some jungle disease. The primal nature of it all seemed to satisfy something in him—a stripped-down exercise that determined who would survive.

We spent weeks at the edge of our backyard, down in the bowled-out depression, where we used the wrought-iron fence of the cemetery as one rope and landscaping timbers as the others. It was our training camp. What we were training for wasn't clear, but we would be ready, prepared for any kind of attack from bears or Arabs or imposing fathers. When we went to school, we wore the bruises and cuts like badges, and when the other kids asked us what had happened we shrugged them off and smirked like they were stupid shits, nudges, all of them. Our muscles went taut as we sweated out the pudding cups and grape sodas, and Charley began to resemble one of our skinned cats—all rib cage and pale flesh and sinewy muscle clinging to an undersized skeleton. Our arms lengthened from the constant torque, our joints loosening up. I twisted my hips like my father told me, bobbed my head, weaved around Charley's haymakers, and dropped a stiff jab or full overhand right often enough that it was clear I was in charge, that Charley was the nudge.

"New game," Charley said when he had tired of straight boxing that he clearly wasn't winning. He dropped a two-by-eight onto the ground and walked it like a plank. "Get on."

We threw leather on the two-by-eight. If you accidentally stepped off, the other guy got a free shot to the body. If you got knocked off, it meant a free shot to the face. If you stepped off on your own, which almost never happened, you got punched in the dick.

Charley rarely backed up. He liked to swim in deep, taking shots to the nose, hoping to land a bare knuckle on my ribs. But I pawed at him with my longer arms, keeping him at a distance, waited for him to commit so that I could belt him with an overhand right.

We threw leather in the dark, that being most of the time in Cut Bank. Either we had short winter days, or the mountains blocked the sun. The light on the back porch was far away from our ring, and by the time it filtered down, it was pale. But through it, we could see each other's eyes, Charley's always flickering like a predator.

When winter landed early, we pulled on our Carhartt chore coats, steam funneling from our heads, and we threw more leather. The padding in the gloves went hard with the cold, and felt like cinder block slamming on our temples. Our free hands struck harder too, like frozen T-bones, though to punch with the bare hand in the cold hurt more than the damage it delivered. We slipped from frost on the board often, and the free shots piled up. Still, neither of us stepped off the board on purpose, knowing that a free shot to our frozen, shriveled dicks in that kind of cold might just jam the whole package up into our small intestines and truly turn us into nudges.

In March of the year we turned sixteen, when we'd been throwing the leather for more than a year, Charley got himself kicked out of school.

I arrived halfway through, never saw how it started. All the versions had him standing in the locker bay between classes, his arm hanging from Carla Depusio, a thoroughly unattractive girl who wore tight shirts and lived down the street. This was around the time I'd nailed Charley with a bare-hand left cross that sliced through his eye. The eyeball bulged out, and the cracked cut refused to close in the cold, just seeped a tea-colored liquid, and so he resembled some menacing mugger, always eyeball-fucking you.

From there, things went cloudy. Everyone claimed to have seen it firsthand, that it was the craziest shit they'd ever seen. The guys tended to claim Charley was a bad dude, a fucking hero. That dude could skin a bear with a spoon, they said. The girls shook their heads and said it didn't matter—he was an animal who belonged in the wild.

Max Woods, a nice enough kid who lived in a two-story with vinyl siding and wore braces and started as a forward on the basketball team, told Charley to leave Carla alone. Some versions had him asking like a nice boy, being chivalrous, saving the young girl from the wolf. Other versions, though, had him demanding, looming over Charley to his full six-foot-plus. However it started, Max ended up raising his fists, and Charley went berserk. He hit Max six times before anyone knew what was happening. I got there just in time to see him timber Max and then pounce on him, dropping fists and elbows, mauling him until he was punching a bloody stump for a face, and through the shouts and moans what rose was the sound of Charley thumping on Max, like the dull thud of a rubber mallet pounding on a decomposing log. He kept punching. Teeth clinked onto the floor and his braces broke loose and jammed through his lips, hung there like dental floss. Carla tried to pull him off, and he backfisted her in the temple. When Charley finally stood up, his knees a dark purple red, Max Woods had swallowed two teeth the doctors had to wait for him to shit out.

Charley never bothered to tell me his full version. He merely claimed that the bitch had it coming, though I never knew who exactly he meant. "Besides," he said, "school is for nudges." It was fine; he needed to train. He was going for the gold gloves now. He'd tasted combat blood, and he needed more. Maybe he'd go box in the marines too. But his ego outgrew his muscles. Charley was a tough kid, but he was no pugilist.

My father thumped Charley when he found out. He wasn't an educated kind of man, but his kids didn't need to be getting booted out of school. Just because we were near-on the border didn't mean we had to act like some bear-poaching Canadians who belonged up in Sweet Grass.

Charley told him to piss off, go bully his own son. I wanted to step in between them, act logical for once, but there was no way for my father to get his justice and Charley to avoid being a nudge. We all knew the rules to these games.

My father thumped him more then, got really rough. He tossed Charley up against the cemetery fence, kicked in his ribs. He picked up one of our jousting brooms and caned his back while Charley writhed on the frozen ground. "Should I still piss off?" my father said.

Charley coughed. "Shit, yes, you should."

The thumping continued with steel-toes to the gut and hard, loud slaps to the face, slaps that left red hand-shaped splotches. Charley pulled himself up by the fence, wobbled there, waiting for my father to keep hitting him. Eventually, my father quit. He threw his hands in the air, grunted, and stomped off to the house, as if defeated because Charley outlasted him.

So Charley stayed home and ate bologna sandwiches with extra mustard while I went to school and tried to earn Bs from teachers who shot me dirty looks like I was some sort of accomplice. But then Charley told me that if he was going to train proper, he needed someone to spar with. I resisted at first, having a bit more fear of authority than he did, but I agreed to stay home a couple days a week and train with him.

We stole Starla's couch cushions and taped them around an aspen for a heavy-bag. When our bare hands broke open from scraping too much, we doused them in snow and switched places. When we'd punched all the stuffing from the cushions, I stole new ones from the school library and tied them up as replacements.

Starla peeked her head out the back door one morning and watched us on the two-by-eight for a minute. She looked over to her cushions wrapped around the tree. "You boys should probably get to school," she said.

Charley looked up at her without moving. "Piss off," he said. "We are at school." Then he turned back to me, and we threw the leather.

She stayed inside after that, watching her soap operas and smoking her menthols.

With no school to punctuate our leather throwing or our new games, Charley started to run wild. He disappeared for longer stretches and returned with scratches on his face and painful looking limps. He talked back to Starla more when my father wasn't around. And at night, when we used to sit in our room and debate our scenarios, he shadowboxed in the foggy backyard light, the tombstones of the cemetery rising up behind him like giant obelisks with long shadows that pointed toward the forest.

One morning, I woke and looked out the window to see him hopping tombstones. He jumped from one to the other without touching the ground like some sinister slackliner who'd lost his rope.

"New game," he told me. "Something I can play while you're at school or sleeping away your life like a nudge."

"Charley," I said and stayed on our side of the fence.

"Don't go puss on me now, Jack," he said. "Go get the gloves, we'll throw the leather like this. None of your dodging nonsense this way."

He grinned. I told him I didn't think so.

"What's with you?" he said. "You're going soft on me."

I told him to piss off, and I walked back to the house to get ready for school.

That night at dinner, I could tell he was still angry with me. I'd broken our pact, drawn a line in the sand that said I'd gone far enough and he was on his own. He clanked dishes together, slopped his cream chicken down so it splattered, and slammed his glass down every time he drank. My father was still gone, working late that night, and Charley knew he was the only man around.

"Would you please settle down?" Starla asked and exhaled her cigarette. "You'll break my dishes that way."

"Piss off," Charley said and glared at his plate.

We sat quietly for a while again, an angry, awkward silence.

Then Starla said, "I saw you out in that cemetery this morning. You need to stay out of there."

"Or what?" Charley said very quickly, too quickly.

"Your father's buried out there. It's not some place for you to practice acting like a jumping frog."

"I should've left a fat boot print on his grave," Charley said. "I'll make sure to do that tomorrow."

Then Starla stood up and smacked Charley in the face. It cracked loudly, but it couldn't have hurt much. It was more of a gesture than a punishment and felt like a piece of theater, something Starla had planned for so long that when she finally did, it seemed forced.

For a moment Charley was too stunned to do anything. He took short, shallow breaths and touched his face. And then he leapt across the table, scattered the dishes onto the floor and toppled the chairs, and started whaling on his mother. He went off, thumped on her until she was a bloody, moaning pile of human, her cigarette still somehow clamped in her jaw, still smoking. When I finally managed to pull him off, she made no movements, just moaned as the smoke rose from her as if she were starting to cremate.

Charley stared down at her and then looked up at me. His breathing quickened as if he just realized what he'd done and what that meant when my father got home. "Shit!" he said. He shuffled off, grabbed his Winchester and his pack, and disappeared through the cemetery and into the woods.

I carried Starla over to the couch, laid her down, covered her with an old afghan so she'd stay warm while she squinted at her soap operas. I found myself tending to her, even lighting her cig-arettes, somehow proud of her for what she'd done because she must have known how Charley would react.

"That's it," my father said when he got home that night, and he didn't speak about it anymore. I was scared for Charley, and I kept my eyes peeled for vultures, wondering if perhaps that was the better way to go.

When Charley emerged six days later, gaunt and pale, he looked like some extinct species rediscovered. He picked his way through the cemetery and hopped the low fence. My father and I had been in the backyard, pulling icicles from the moldy soffit, and Charley must have seen us, waited until we were outside. He carried his father's Winchester on one shoulder, the chamber levered open, and on the other hung the rusty linkages of chain.

My father slowly unlatched his thick leather belt and stripped it out of his Carhartts. It was a menacing image, a Cut Bank knight drawing his sword, and I knew Charley was in for it. But he strode right past us as if indifferent to our existence, and I saw the dangling jaws of a grizzly trap hanging over his shoulder.

Charley disappeared into the garage and emerged with his hatchet. He pried open the jaw of the trap and set the trigger. He stepped away, looped the chain links around the cemetery fence, and latched the steel carabiner. Then he dropped our two-by-eight in front of the trap, like a plank descending into the leviathan's throat. He stepped on, right in front of the trap, waited.

My father and I stared. Neither of us moved.

Charley raised his little fists. "New game," he said.

Still we didn't move.

He shuffled back, his heel bumping the trap. "Get on, Jack," he said.

My father looked to me, motioned toward the two-by-eight with the hand that held his dangling belt, folded over onto itself. I hesitated, not knowing if I was doing my father's bidding or Charley's.

"Don't be a nudge," Charley said.

I stepped on. Charley glared at me like I was the enemy, like I was prey. His bloodshot eyes bulged. We had no leather, just our cracked, frozen fists. We all knew how it would end, knew that Charley couldn't out-box me.

Charley attacked, came at me, and I bent my lead knee and snapped a jab. I pawed at him, didn't let him inside. He slipped off the frozen board and I cracked him in the ribs. He came at me again, and I caught him with a straight right, flattened his nose, and it started to pour blood into his mouth. I waited on him to attack.

"Come on!" he said. "Come at me. Don't be a nudge!" He had to breathe through his mouth and spit the blood onto the snow.

I pushed forward, swaying as I dropped lefts to the face and rights to the body, and Charley fell back. His heel pushed onto the trap again, nudged it back. He stood there, covered up his bloody face, and I sliced through his arms with an uppercut to his open jaw.

When he fell back, his right leg stomped into the bear trap as if on purpose, and the teeth sliced into him without a sound. No crack or thud, just the soft whisper of a fillet knife being thrown into wet sand. Charley fell immediately. It sliced and he fell like a switch had been tripped. He wailed, yelled out the kind of pitiful shriek normally reserved for the far reaches of the wilderness.

My father and I didn't move. We knew his leg was broken, that he'd limp from now on. Charley howled and clutched the cemetery fence. I'm sure all my father saw was justice stolen from him again. A pathetic kid cuffed to a bear clamp, crying for his mother. But I saw more than that. I saw a mean kid who had sacked a trap from a bear's clutches, and for a long time I stood in between Charley and my father and didn't move to help while he moaned and fought his way up the fence like a wild animal thrashing against his shackles.

Evolution of the Mule

There is drought here, always drought. For ten years it has cemented the earth into a vast cracked slab, horizon to horizon. There is no more prairie grass, only towering squalls of topsoil that lurch across the land like hulking phantoms, vengeful and clumsy. There is the long quiet, the desperate wait for rain.

Nights, the boy, Wiley, lies next to his sister on their cot in the kitchen and listens to the pattering on the tin roof, wishing it were rain but knowing it is only a blowing mimic of dirt rain. He will scrape it from the windowpanes in the morning, from the pits between his toes, from his eyeballs, which are always scratched red. He is a slight, towheaded child, nearly fourteen but so quiet he seems younger. He carries his shoes as often as he wears them and always remembers to leave the last sip of water in his cup for Helen, his sister. She is the ornery one, two years younger and likely to kick his shins just before a foot race.

From the lone bedroom room barks the rough animal sounds, the uncle atop their mother, his sister. Wiley tries not to picture it, his uncle's unshaven face, his mother's clenched cheeks, but the groans rattle through the walls. Even the smell reaches him, the reek of hot sweat and body oil, of the uncle loosing himself into her and then collapsing. In the morning, the mother will emerge first, always, and she will wake Wiley and then Helen with gentle rubs on their backs and shoulders. Time to see the sun, my pea-cocks, she says to them. Her eyes are sunken and empty, as if their sockets are a size too large.

The father is dead eight years now, smallpox, and they have lived with the uncle this whole time. He has a long, snouty face, all nose and Adam's apple and heavy stubble. He is a harsh man, hateful of all who draw too near, to Wiley most of all. He works the farm quickly with slipshod fixes, leaving sloppy hammer dents and cockeyed fence posts. He reads poorly and neglects the almanac planting schedules, and the yields suffer. He insists on strict replanting each year, and the parched soil slowly turns to charcoal. When he is angry, he boxes Wiley's ears red, and if the boy cries out, he shims a screwdriver under the boy's thumbnail. You must be strong for this world, he says, as if his cruelties are lessons on manhood. He shows Wiley his own thumbs; the dark stains beneath his nails also bulge as if enormous splinters need exhumed. He gawks at Helen in a way that none of them are able to ignore. Wiley is far too scrawny to intervene.

They are beggars squatting on his lifeless land. It is all scalded, its minerals devoured by the wind. Sixty-two acres suitable for planting, most far above the water table. Only the barnyard well reaches it, a narrow socket plunging down to the cold water that they are told to ration. The water is more important than your blood, the uncle reminds them often. No irrigation trenches, and so they plant sweet sorghum and broom corn, both hardy plants with tiny finger roots, and this gives them grain and sugar stalks.

The mother helps harvest bushels of the red grains, flours much into a sorghum porridge and sometimes a dense flatbread. The sweet stalks his uncle feeds into the mule-driven press for the sugar. The mule is his most valued possession because, like all of its kind, it is sterile. When it dies, there is no replacement. He boils the sugar down into blackstrap molasses. Half of this syrup they send west to Denver for quick profits. The other half is distilled into a dark rum that he casks and displays on the front porch with a sign: *Fresh Sorghum Rum, $6/gallon.* The salesmen and grain haulers passing through on their way to Denver slowly bleed the cask, fill water jugs and coffee cans, which are sold for a quarter extra. If the rum has not sold by winter, the uncle loads it onto the ancient Hudson and drives the length of the county, stays gone several days, stopping at each door to hock it for firewood and seeds and oil to last them through winter. He takes with him all but a dozen matches, much of the flour, even the children's shoes. His family must not flee. The mule he leaves behind, and Wiley is to feed it before breakfast, before dinner.

With the uncle gone Wiley squares his shoulders, sets box traps for muskrats and prairie dogs, guts and cleans them, leaving his pale hands heavy with blood and stink that he cannot wash off. He brings them home to his mother, who fries them in the skillet.

They do not sit in silence at the kitchen table, and his mother's eyes do not hang so low. They wait for the uncle to return.

You should hack off his mule's hooves while he's gone, Helen says to Wiley. The mother scowls, but then turns away and smiles, and Wiley laughs, and they all laugh. We should mince them up and sprinkle his porridge, she says, and they continue to laugh, though Helen was making no joke. She has planned much worse things for her uncle.

The uncle claimed once that his bond with the mother is of necessity and not pleasure. He wished it could be another way, but they must survive. He pointed to Wiley's narrow shoulders and bent posture. If the mule dies, where will we be then? he said. We must grow the family. How much can I do alone? But there is no new child, and it is not merely hope that steers him on all this time.

The uncle is gone longer this year, nearly two weeks now peddling the rum, and supplies run low. The wheat flour can be measured by the spoonful. The mother mashes the last of the sorghum grain and bakes a waffled cake that cuts their gums. For several days they eat spoonfuls of molasses atop Wiley's fried vermin, and this hides the gamey bitterness. But the molasses bucket runs low, so the mother brews bitter dark coffee to help mask the flavor and swell their stomachs, and her children do not complain about this or anything.

Nights, when the temperature plummets, the mother sets outside all four mugs, filled with water, places sticks in each, so that when it freezes, the iced sticks might resemble real food that can be held and chewed. She prays each evening that someday her children will know the taste of ice cream, the scent of muskmelon.

Wiley must trot across the frozen ground with bare feet to feed the mule from the dwindling baskets of sorghum feed. Often the animal eats from its own dung pile, burrowing its snout and finding undigested grains. Wiley scratches the mule's ears, unable to dislike the animal simply because it belongs to his uncle. It is a stupid and helpless thing and so perfectly good-natured, staid from breeding methods and unable to escape its destiny as a muscled serf.

Evenings the mother and children play musical chairs in the kitchen, burning the fire low until it is only glowing coals that they rake and draw the bellows on for hours, and they feel as if they are stealing heat this way. The mother hums a tune as they step around the twin chairs. Helen times the endings well, managing to step on Wiley's feet or tug on his belt loops or dive lengthwise across both chairs as the song ends, and Wiley always waits too long. She feels a power in this, and Wiley does not complain or stymie her but laughs at each maneuver, not simply because he loves her but also because her freckled, ornery face stuns him. She is a beautiful little thing, cherubic and effectual, and Wiley suffers this like a swelling and private plague.

Outside, the winter has descended upon them, the cutting winds unravelling like a great rug, shaken from hundreds of miles away, so barren and free of clutter is the landscape. The dust kicks up, frozen and painful, pelting their faces. When they stand outside, backs to these gales, it nearly bends them over, like field-weary slaves yielding to the long whips of the wind.

The supplies are nearly gone, and the uncle has still not returned. Maybe someone shot him in his stupid monkey brain,

Helen says. Pow! she says, and mimics a pistol shot to the temple. Wiley smiles at her, and yet he knows the awful truth, that his uncle is repugnant but vital. Wiley cannot work the farm alone, not with his narrow shoulders, his bony forearms.

Helen flashes Wiley her thin smile, has him guide the prize mule onto the front porch, which sits not thirty paces off the roadway to Denver. She latches a rope to its bridle and onto the rope she slides a small golden ring—the father's ring—stolen from the uncle's chest. She ties the rope's other end to the support post, and so the ring dangles there between the two like a golden tightrope walker. From the mule's bare back she hangs a sign: *Unstring the Golden Ring and Keep It! $1/try!*

You can't get the ring off, Wiley tells her very simply. Not without unhitching the mule.

They won't know that, Helen says. They'll think it's a puzzle. And they'll be anxious to stop and stretch their legs.

They'll figure it out.

But, she says, we'll already have their dollar by then. She pauses, scowls at him. Do you want to eat muskrat guts all winter?

The salesmen, legs weary and nearly petrified from the road, pull onto the packed dirt circle drive. They step out, arch their backs, grunt. They are men, all of them, mostly young men, and many are overweight from the long miles spent traveling. They wear ironed shirts and short ties, and their Florsheims are without scuffs.

Most wink at Wiley and Helen, offer their dollars freely when they see the children's red and shredded feet, and they understand they are making a small donation. Helen sees this soon and feels no guilt. Hold still! she tells Wiley, and she rips apart the shoulder seam from his shirt. She slices his cheek with her fingernail, smears the blood into his dirty face. She tears the bottom hem from her dress, flashing more of her skinny legs. She wipes mule dung on their faces and necks. They are miniature hobos, starved and reeking.

They earn their dollars, and Helen tells Wiley to ignore the sad looks. You do what you must, she says, sounding very old and wise, like the mother. These men offer their dollars, and she sends Wiley off to the small store two miles distant to buy wheat flour and coffee and, once, two strips of bacon, which burns down Wiley's neck because he eats it so quickly. He wants to vomit it up just to eat it again.

One salesman, younger than the others, with a doughy, fresh face, spends a quarter hour with the roped ring. He slides it back and forth from the rigging to the post, thinking. He carves the air with squiggly lines, as if parsing an equation. He bends the rope over onto itself, tries tying off a Flemish knot. He checks the ring and the rigging and the bit for secret spring-loaded clasps.

It's impossible, the man says finally.

Wiley looks to Helen, feels his abdomen go cold.

I'll have my dollar back now.

The children sit still. Helen shakes her head.

The man shouts down at Wiley, Where's your father?

Dead.

What about your mother?

She's dead too, says Helen. We live with our uncle who collects swords and cannons, and one time he stabbed a man in the brain for asking a question about sausage gravy.

The man steps toward Helen. Wiley moves between them.

Boy! the man snaps.

Wiley stands still, and when the man takes another step, he latches onto the man's leg, bites through his wool slacks near his knee and deep into his flesh until he hits bone, drawing out hot blood that stains the creases between his teeth. The man yelps. He hammers down onto Wiley's skinny neck. Helen runs up and stomps his foot, hard, and the man falls down the porch steps. He slithers on the ground and moans.

He drives off. Wiley wipes the blood from his teeth, feels where one tooth has broken off, and realizes it must still be in the man's thigh. He rubs on the broken tooth, its rough edge, spits.

Helen smiles at him, guides him to the porch steps where he

sits. She inspects his neck, which will blush with purple and yellow overnight. She wraps her arms around his torso. We sure earned that one, she says.

Wiley leans back into her, breathes deeply her scent. He noses into her neck until she stands and backs away.

The long-armed man appears on the horizon that evening, nearly three weeks since the uncle has been gone, when the winter has softened and the snow has melted. He walks slowly, no car or horse, just an ancient, sun-scalded Stetson, knee-high boots, and a Winchester repeater poking from his canvas pack.

His arms dangle low, nearly to his knees when his posture slackens, hang there as if ready to lash fools with, and he looks not unlike an ape. His hands too are massive, his fat fingers long enough to wrap around a telephone pole, it seems to the children. He is not a large man, not six foot, not two hundred pounds, but his gait is lumbering like a silverback. His face is splotchy from the sun and scarred with deep pockmarks, and the children think he has been tortured by nasty men with knives, but the blots are clearly from a bout of smallpox.

The man strides up to the porch, squints at the sign. He says nothing and does not look at the children, does not seem to even notice them. Helen punches Wiley's shoulder and gestures toward the well, and Wiley scampers off to bring the man a full ladle. He drinks it slowly, making no noise. Wiley stares at the rifle in his pack, at his dangling arms.

When the man speaks, his voice is soft like a child's, not impolite but lean, fragmentary. That barn free for the night? he says, gesturing.

Wiley looks to Helen, and she nods without thinking. The man removes his hat and walks toward the barn. His steps are short and timid, as if he has gravel in his boots. He disappears into the dark barn.

The mother scolds Wiley for allowing the man to stay. What were you thinking? she says. A strange man when your uncle is gone? And with a gun! Wiley does not defend the decision or argue. He does not claim that it was Helen who invited the man. She is unused to strange faces. Even those of the salesmen driving past seem familiar. But a man with no car or horse is not to be trusted.

Wiley is fascinated. He has not known many men and does not remember much of his father beyond the sweet smell of his chewing tobacco and his rattly laugh that rumbled through the depths of his gullet.

He bets Helen that the long-armed man is an escaped convict from the prison in Wichita.

Then how does he have a gun?

He crushed a man's skull, Wiley says. A police man. Crushed his skull and stole his gun.

Then why didn't he steal the car, too?

He thinks for a moment, looks at his dirty bare feet. He doesn't know how to drive, he says.

Are you kidding me? With those arms? I bet he could drive a car and juggle swords at the same time.

Wiley glares at her. He knows in a backward way that she is the clever one and that this is no time for imagination. But he wants only to impress her.

He stands in the shadow of the barn, peers between siding slats, watches the ape man. He undresses slowly, revealing heavy tattoos notched with matching scars, as if an outline has been carved and then colored. They are long, winding patterns, never crisscrossing, and they unfurl about his shoulder blades, down his arms, wrap around his torso and back, all of them billowing, crawling across his body like long arms reaching for things unseen. They engulf his shoulders in great waves, wrap about his pale torso with no end. And underneath the rippling, tattooed scars there are the pox craters, hundreds of them, dormant and veiled.

The man does not look up but speaks in his slow, lilting drawl: You should bring that mule in before it storms.

Wiley feels like an animal caught in a live trap. He does not move. He has not noticed the sky darkening or the clouds swirling above in a dizzying rush, and the appearance of the ape man excites him more than even the storm.

The man removes his pants, revealing pale white cheeks. His tattoos and scars halt at the waist, as if they are imprinted upon a body sleeve that can be removed.

Quickly now, the man says.

Wiley runs off toward the porch and the mule. He drags the animal away from its leftover shitpile, back toward the barn. He tethers it near the ape man. The mule begins to buck and bray because it feels the looming storm in its bones, and Wiley scratches its snout and its floppy ears until the animal calms.

The clouds burst, explode open with a thunder crack, muddying the dirt barnyard into a vast pool. Helen jumps from the porch and into the deluge, waving her arms and kicking her legs until she tumbles into the mud. She carves mud angels in it, laughs, and she does not feel her skin tighten with the intense cold of the winter rain.

Wiley watches her dance and fall and spin as if she is wrestling the rain. Her thin ripped dress clings to her stomach, revealing the hollow imprint of her belly button. He has forgotten the ape man, who stands behind him and stares without blinking. Wiley steps out in to the rain, where the fat drops are much colder than he expected, like small splotches of venom burning his bare skin, and he cannot fathom how Helen ignores it. When she sees him there, she rushes at him, tackles him to the mud and then cackles. And Wiley does not notice the cold then as she squeezes his stomach and growls, pretends to hammer his chest with her small fists. She pins him to the mud with her knees and batters his shoulders, grabs his head and smears it into the sloppy mud. They laugh and tumble in the mud. She rolls him to his stomach, stands, and then pounces again, driving her elbow into his back, and they laugh there in the mud yard while the ape man watches and pets the mule.

The night freezes the deluge, and the mud wrestling pit in the barnyard hardens into lumpy waves where Wiley and Helen have carved their imprints. If the uncle saw such a thing, he would grab his screwdriver and call for Wiley, but the uncle is still gone.

The mother wakes first to gather her children's wet clothes and drape them near the fire. The dense mud is still stuck in between the cotton fibers, and they will never get any cleaner than they are now, but she does not worry over this, knowing that such a storm happens only rarely, knowing that her children do not laugh and play often enough.

Wiley wakes and trots to the barn in only his jockey shorts, leads the mule to the front porch and tethers him there to do his ring dance so they might eat breakfast. Helen emerges with the golden ring and slides it onto the rope. She sits on the porch steps, her tired eyes cast downward, her thin arms clutching her stomach. They sit quietly and drink from their mugs of water until their bellies bloat.

The fierce cold has returned, but Wiley and Helen sit on the porch and wait for their prey to arrive and make their donations so that they might scamper off and buy oats or wheat. The mule, which usually eats before the humans, noses through a day-old dung pile. Wiley is so hungry that he considers, for a moment, picking through it with the mule.

The ape man emerges from the barn, fully dressed with his pack and rifle. He wanders toward the front porch, and Wiley runs off to fetch him water again. The ape man does not stare at Helen. He watches the mule as it looms there, unmoving and stupid.

Would you like to give it a go? Helen asks.

The ape man squints down at her. Is the ring real gold? he asks.

Helen nods that yes, it is, though she does not know this for certain.

Wiley returns from the well, and the ape man drinks deeply. He is a menacing presence, and Wiley tries to stare through his clothes to see his scarred tattoos again, but he can see only those markings which reach up, clutching his neck like flickering flames.

No one has done it yet, Helen says.

The ape man reaches into his jacket pocket, pulls out four quarters, drops them into Helen's palm. Helen looks over to Wiley and smiles. They can both taste the warm bread they will eat soon, once the ape man has given up and moved on.

The ape man does not test the rope or slide the ring toward the rigging. He sets his pack onto the frozen ground, slowly loads his Winchester. He levels it to the mule's head and squeezes off a single round.

The mule collapses into a heap. Steam pulses from it. Its muscles jerk and twitch, unshod hooves knocking on porch boards. The mother bursts through the front door and stops when she sees the ape man with his rifle. Helen cowers behind, and for a moment the world idles, and they fear what is next.

The mule's legs seize, and all goes quiet. Then the ape man sheaths the rifle back into his pack. He walks to the pile of dead mule, bends, examines the bridle and the ring on the rope, which is still attached.

I'll be back through for my ring, he says, and he leaves.

In three days the uncle returns. He has still not traded all the rum, and so he is drunk from the last measure of it, the congealed traces at the cask bottom which he must chew on like fat. The dead mule lingers on the front porch, and he sees this first. Even the wilting brain has been left alone because they are afraid to move anything. It is Wiley who must tell him what happened, how he could not protect the uncle's prize mule. It is all his fault, was all his idea. He knows the mule was sterile and there is no replacing it. He has considered running away from here because the uncle's vengeance will be gruesome. Surely it will leave him with a limp or blurred vision or without thumbs. Perhaps all of those things. But it is his job to be the family shield, to absorb twice the punishment so that his sister, his lovely smart sister, will avoid disfigurations, will marry a sweet man who can buy her shoes and parasols and fresh milk. He is not a stupid boy, has known for years how things must be.

The uncle thinks Wiley lies about the ape man. Stupid boy! he shouts and squeezes his wrist, hauls him into the workshop. Tell me what happened!

Wiley repeats the story. He leaves nothing out. He tells the uncle about the ring game they used to survive while he was away for so long and about the salesmen who stopped. The uncle smacks and kicks him for this, and Helen runs toward her brother, paws at the uncle to make him stop. The uncle turns to her, but Wiley pushes her away and says that some of the salesmen stopped for longer, some even visited the mother. Inside, he says. At this, the uncle's face hardens. He snatches Wiley up by the armpit, driving an elbow into his neck. He slams Wiley's face onto the workbench, and the boy's orbital bone cracks. He yelps. The uncle jams a knuckle into Wiley's temple, slowly, increasing the pressure until it seems his brain will explode like the mule's. Wiley cannot even manage a moan. A croak trickles from his the back of his throat, and gobs of saliva drain onto the workbench.

What happened? the uncle demands, but Wiley cannot answer. His boiling blood pumps through his cracked cheek and throbbing eye. Thick drops form in his tear duct as if he is crying blood. Then the sound of the uncle rattling in the toolbox, finding the flat-blade screwdriver, the knowledge of what is to come.

Then Helen is standing over him. His vision is blurry. He paws at his face, which is puffy and raw. His broken eye socket has not been reset. He feels the bandages cinching his thumbs, feels them pulse against the swelling.

Helen lifts his head, pours hot sorghum rum down his throat. He swallows and coughs. My eye, he says.

I know, she says. Don't worry, she says.

The mother's flesh grays nearly overnight. Her spine slumps, and she no longer wakes first with her peacocks. Some quiet plague has infected them, and the mother's limbs swell and darken with a brutal malignancy. Helen bends over her, sleeping little. She worries not just of her mother's condition but of her own fate if she dies.

The uncle carries on as before. He does not speak to Wiley, though he does tend to the mother when she coughs and moans during the night. They all seem to understand that she will die soon, though no one knows what to call her disease and no one speaks of it. It is not an uncommon thing in such a place to grow sick suddenly and die of a nameless contamination.

For Wiley, it is as if some hulking and unseen banshee has descended upon his world. The uncle's torture is not new, nor is the threat of the mother's death. He paws at his pinched socket often. The eyelid will not close fully now, and even his hearing has grown strained from it, the vibrations of sound plunging into a hollow conduit and then rattling at the base of his neck. More than all this, it is the thought of the of ape man returning that tortures him. Even the uncle, who claims he does not believe the story, does not touch the rotting mule.

The carcass festers on the porch, freezing and thawing along with the weather's fluctuations. Patches of its mane still grip the neck, but much of its hair has fallen off and sticks between the cracks of the floorboards. Vultures have eaten most of its paunch, ripped strings of its bowels out and flown away with them in their beaks like fat worms. The reek of it chokes the house and even the barnyard. The golden ring still hangs from the rope, though it would take only a small tug to free it from the mule's bit.

Early March and Wiley walks the long rows and plants the grains with the uncle. The soil remains hard, and they must till much of it with a spud bar since they no longer have the mule to drag the plow. They carve long rows of cockeyed V's, trickle sorghum seeds, and cover them. And they wait, long hours they wait for green leaves to sprout and for the ape man to appear on the horizon.

Mid-spring, and the mother wilts and dies. It is slow and loud. For weeks no one sleeps at night because her moans rattle even the spoons and forks in the drawer. Her gray skin yellows and opens as if gangrene speeds through her veins. Helen does not leave her often, only to fill buckets of cold water and to clean puss from the rags that bathe her forehead. She listens to the mother's rattly breathing when she sleeps, and this is when the uncle descends.

We need fresh bread, he says to her. I need my shirt washed, he says. Come sit with me, he says, and pats the lumpy cushion next to him.

Go torture a scarecrow! she shouts at him, and he leaves her to tend to the mother, though his eyes always trace back toward her. She can feel his eyes, and she knows the way of things in this world, the way of replacements, and his desire for more field hands.

They bury the mother at sunrise in early spring when the frost has withdrawn for the season. Wiley fashions a headstone by breaking off barn siding and cinching it with twine. He carves into it the word *Mother*, digs a trench, and anchors it into the ground above her. Then they all stand and look down at it, and no one speaks. Helen grips Wiley's hand, and the silence infects them until they are all afraid to move.

That night there are no animal noises from the bedroom, but they hear the uncle's sobs. He has shown no regret in front of them, no trace of sadness, but the awful tempest within him unleashes with the loneliness. He has lost so much with her. For a moment Helen feels for him, the howling and tortured beast that cannot not be domesticated by this world. He has no place but on his lonely dust farm, no capacity to comprehend the fundamental order he has disturbed.

The harvest is slow in the summer as Wiley and the uncle must scythe and hack the heavy stalks and drag them by hand. Wiley replaces the mule at the sorghum press, circling for long hours as the uncle feeds the brambles in to be mashed. The orbital bone will not set properly, and so his face is locked in a perpetual and lopsided grimace. Even his smile appears sinister, like some malevolent marionette with its strings drawn too tight.

For three years they carry on this way, Wiley growing strong, growing weary. He does not speak of the ape man or of his delayed return, but he thinks of it daily and fears both his appearance and his absence.

Maybe he died, Helen says at breakfast.

Wiley glares at her and says nothing. He sits quietly, looks down. We need more coffee, he says.

His shoulder muscles bulge now from the long workdays with no mule, and his forearms have tanned and grown veiny. Long scars carve his hands and up to his elbows, scars from working sharp tools beyond his capacities. And he has grown serious, agonies scored about his face, and for this, the uncle commends him. This, he says, is how we become capable men. It was the same for me. One day, he says, you'll have your own mule, and the burdens will ease.

Helen has grown tall and thin. Her face has hardened, and though she is not beautiful, she is still too beautiful for such a place. Her wiry muscles also stretch as she works the field next to Wiley. He will rarely let her from his sight. It is only Wiley and his thick muscles, his glower, that keeps the uncle away from their bedroom at night.

The mule carcass has melted away, and all that remains are the bones: ribcage and legs and enormous hips, untouched all this time. The rope has detached from the bridle, and so nothing keeps the ring shackled to it. The ape man's plan has worked, and yet he does not return. The uncle avoids the porch because this would acknowledge the truth of Wiley's story, but he does not order the bones cleaned up.

And they wait for the ape man. It is four years, then five, and still Wiley knows he will return. He must return. The uncle still pretends there is no ape man, but in all this time he has not removed the mule bones, has not ordered Wiley to do so. Still they cling to the front porch. They have yellowed, and dirt cakes into the eye sockets.

The uncle has withered. Whether from the endless toil or the thought of the ape man or the death of his sister, it is hard to explain. He sleeps late and eats little, and when Wiley needs an extra hand, he shouts in to Helen. When the uncle drinks too much sorghum rum, Wiley smacks his temples red with the flat of his callused hands. You drink our dinner, you fool! he shouts at the uncle. Helen must sit between them at dinner as Wiley stares at the uncle, seething. More than once she has pulled her brother away for fear he would kill the uncle with his fists.

The absent ape man breeds a meanness in Wiley that was never there before. Every day he has not returned, Wiley's shoulders coil tighter until he snaps even at Helen. He is a hulking specter of the towheaded boy he was, scowling and clenching a cob pipe between his yellowed teeth. He glowers down at Helen, and it is not unlike the looks the uncle gave her years earlier. She fears what the world makes him into. Wiley claims to want only enough saved income to purchase an old tractor—an Allis-Chalmers or Farmall or even a newer Deutz. He will never buy a mule. He is convinced they might undo the land's blight, and their own, with modern implements. Helen thinks he is perhaps correct in this, that the endless toil and inch-thick calluses have animalized him. He growls more than he speaks, often eats while standing and with his dirty hands.

Seven years after the ape man, the uncle dies. He has lost nearly half his body weight, and his knuckles bulge. He drinks much of the season's rum, and Wiley allows it because it pacifies him.

Before he dies, the uncle waves Wiley over. They sit at the kitchen table in summer, but it is chilly, and Wiley stokes the coals. The uncle and Wiley sit quietly for a while, the uncle drawing his thin, wheezing breaths, and Wiley inhaling the heavy plumes from his cob pipe. The wind gusts through the siding and into the kitchen, swirling dirt about the floorboards.

What did he look like? the uncle asks, and Wiley knows what he means.

Wiley describes the scars and the tattoos. He mentions the pox blemishes. He pauses, and then he describes the ape arms. They dangled, he says, like twine, longer than his legs. He carried a jungle gun, an African thing made for elephants and lions. He was like a circus show, more animal than man. His speech quickens, and he describes the mule's exploding brain, how it burst like a squeezed seed. He has not spoken this many words together in a year. He tells the uncle of the storm the night before and of wrestling Helen in the mud pit.

The uncle smiles at him. He even laughs, though it erupts like a cough. Wiley pulls out a wad of handkerchief, hands it to the uncle.

The uncle coughs blood into the handkerchief. And what if he comes back? he asks. What do you do then?

Wiley has thought of little else for years, but he has no answer and never will. He looks down.

You see? the uncle says. There are worse things out there than me.

He is dead the next day, and they bury him beside the mother. Helen clasps Wiley's thick forearm as they look down at the mounded dirt. Wiley has made no marker for it and has no plans to add one. There are enough remnants of the uncle around them.

Wiley thinks about how they might build another room for the house, another bedroom. Scour the porch clean of mule, wall it in. Buy another cot, a nightstand, an oil lamp. They will sleep in separate rooms and work their hardened farm as they must, behave as they must. How then he might venture out with all their savings, leverage the old Hudson, the farm itself. *Yes, sir*, he'll say, head bent. *The older one there. The '18 Fordson, sir. No, sir, I understand. I'll work the bearings back into shape, sir.* Wiley will return home with their tractor one morning, riding high atop it like a conqueror. He will call out to his sister so she might see his arrival, see as he pulls into the lane, circles a lap around the house, and parks it next to the sorghum press.

The Era of Good Feelings

When my father died, my mother didn't hide her annoyance. "In February?" she said, looking out the back window to the snow-covered plot our family had used for more than a hundred years. "Christ."

"The Garchers have that backhoe," I reminded her. "No one's expecting you to go out there with a spade."

"Which they'll charge us to rent."

She was right about that. The Garchers were our nearest neighbor, four hundred yards to the east. They ran almost six hundred acres, which counted as rich for the area. They made a big show out of eating at the new Applebee's in town. I'd gone to school with Charlie Garcher, a toady, stupid boy who became a toady, stupid man. When I went off to college, he stayed home. When I came back to be a history teacher and help my father run the farm, I returned to student loans and the same flood-prone tract as when I'd left, but Charlie had inherited another four hundred acres and had no loans. It's hard not to resent the fools who succeed because they have no ambition.

"We flat don't have money for a funeral," my mother said.

"We'll figure something out."

"People always say that when they don't know how to figure it out."

I could see she needed to wallow for a while. Despair scabs over grief when we need it to. My mother and father had the kind of marriage where they loved each other, yes, but every year it seemed less relevant. They had a farm to run and bills to pay. Who had time to be in love?

My mother disappeared into the kitchen to cook something we didn't need, and I dialed Charlie Garcher. "Dad died last night," I said.

"Sorry to hear that. Need the backhoe?"

"If it's not too much trouble. Tomorrow probably."

"It's no trouble. Same as usual?" he asked, meaning the rate.

"It's fine, Charlie," I said and hung up.

After that I called my principal, Hal Owens. Hal was a good enough guy. We used to fish crappie together before he became principal. He was from Massachusetts, but he'd been in Ohio for almost twenty years, so people were starting to warm to him. "Don't tell anyone," I said. "I don't want a million phone calls right now."

"Sure, of course," Hal said. "Take a few days. Let them read about it in the paper." He was probably relieved at the thought of me taking a little time off. The week before, one of my American Government students, Cassidey Duluth, barged into the teacher's lounge looking for me, calling me by my first name, Ralph, claiming we had some sort of appointment which we didn't have. Another teacher complained, and word reached Hal. The suggestion of impropriety was strong enough to trigger an investigation, probably because Cassidey was pretty, and pretty people conjure the image of sex just by being present. I found it all very confusing. I hadn't had much more than a whiff of sex in years, not since a short marriage and a long divorce, but if you keep your eyes open in these parts, you can see a storm coming from a long way off.

After I hung up, it occurred to me that my father was still in bed, which is where he died. My mother had found him, stiff and cold, that morning. (She would later admit after a few drinks at the wake that she had suspected he was dead in the middle of the night since he wasn't snoring. *Did you actually fall back to sleep?* I asked her. *I dozed*, she said.) I went out to the barn and unfolded a couple of sawhorses and set an old piece of ply on top. There was a big oil stain on one side, so I flipped it over to the other side, which had a smaller oil stain. Then I went in and pulled my father out of bed and hauled him out to the barn. Rigor mortis had already set in, which made him feel stiff and breakable. I grabbed him up under the armpits and tried to lift him all the way but couldn't. I didn't want to drag him, but that's what I ended up doing, his feet cutting these creases in the snow of the barnyard, which I would stomp over on my way back to the house, hoping my mother wouldn't have to see them. I set him on the piece of ply and shut the barn door. It would stay cold enough for a day.

I went back inside and sat down at the desk with a mug of rye to write his obituary. This was Friday, and the paper ran on Saturday mornings, which meant we could do the funeral and wake Saturday evening.

What did I want to say about my father? *He was a tough old bird*, I wrote at first and then scratched it out because it was stupid cliché. You don't call your father a tough old bird to a town full of tough old birds. I realized that about home the first week I went away to college and was surrounded by suburbanites who thought hay and straw were the same thing and that grocery stores made all their own food on site. I wrote about how he served honorably in the Pacific. *Killed himself many Japs*, I wrote, and then scratched that out too because I thought it was funny in an ironic sort of way that most people would think was serious and patriotic. *Loving father and husband, a man who worked the good earth his whole life.* Truth is, the life of a farmer is all about repetition. You're tethered to the calendar, and you end up in this orbit, and before you know it fifty years have gone by and all that's different is that your barn now has aluminum siding. I wrote down a few more platitudes and gave the information about the wake and the funeral and decided

I needed to stop because it was just too sad how I could hardly hit fifty words for a man who'd lived to eighty.

Things would change now, and it wasn't clear how we'd cover bills. Probably we'd have to lease the land out to Charlie Garcher for nickels on what it was worth, which would allow us to sell off some equipment. That thought burned me up, Garchers running plow on my family's land like a horde of stinking barbarians. My family bought this farm when James Monroe was president. That was called the Era of Good Feelings. In a lot of ways, that was as good as it ever got for a small farmer, 1817 or so, and it's been a humiliating struggle ever since.

It wasn't even noon by this point, and I was thinking of going in to school to teach the last couple bells of the day. I had a nice group for American Government. A few of them would go on to college, and one or two might end up with jobs where they wore collared shirts. Cassidey Duluth wasn't one of them.

I went to the kitchen to check in on my mother. She was frying eggs. "You hungry?"

"No," I said.

A couple minutes later she set an egg sandwich down in front of me, and I ate it mindlessly in about four bites. "I'm going to teach the last couple bells," I told her. "Then I'll see about a casket." The casket was a reach; a headstone was a non-starter.

"We don't have money for that."

"I'll figure something out." I'd learned from my father that if you just order something first and worry about how to pay for it later, the whole situation really becomes somebody else's problem. Who would come repossess a casket?

"I still need to call your brother and tell him."

I hadn't even thought of my brother. He worked at a bank over in Fort Wayne, which meant we didn't know how to talk to each other anymore.

I took the long route to school, which wound me all the way around the Garcher place. I guess I wanted to torture myself.

Charlie himself was out getting the mail at the end of their lane, and he waved at me, so I pulled off for a minute.

"Sorry to hear about the old man," he said. "He was a tough old bird."

"Yeah."

"How's your mother doing?"

"You know how she is. Mostly mad about how expensive it is to die."

"I hear that," Charlie said, which was a stupid thing to say because the only people who'd ever died on him were his in-laws, and they left him four hundred acres and God knows how much cash under the mattress. "You know what you're going to do yet?" he asked, meaning, *could I buy your land out from under you?*

"We'll figure it out after the funeral."

"I'll run the backhoe over tonight," Charlie said. "Then you can use it whenever works for you."

"Thanks again," I said, though what I really meant was *fuck you and your stupid face.* "It really means a lot to us." Maybe flattery would make Charlie think he was letting us use his backhoe for free. I was going make him send me a goddamned bill if he wanted our money so goddamned bad. When I drove off, I made sure to gas it a little extra and kick up the gravel in his lane, which was a stupid little gesture that made me feel awfully good.

I made it to sixth bell a few minutes late and realized I didn't have a lesson planned, so I just told them to use the time as study hall, and I sat there and planned something for American Government. Most of the kids sat there texting, which was against the rules, but I never enforced that one. Running a small farm teaches you never to punch back against technology because technology always wins.

Cassidey was the first one in for seventh bell. She seemed startled when she saw me. "I heard you were absent today."

"I'm here now."

"You look like hell, Ralph."

She was wearing those low-cut Levis that showed her hip

bones, also against schools rules, also not enforced by me. It used to be you never had to think about these sorts of things, but now I wouldn't meet with a student, male or female, unless my door was wide open.

I started my lesson, which was supposed to be about the Wilmot Proviso and the Compromise of 1850, how they bled into the Civil War, but this led me backward to the Missouri Compromise and then all the way to the Treaty of Ghent and how those frameworks really encouraged the settlement of the Ohio River valley. It was enough material for ten lessons, and I was lecturing in a disorganized mess.

"During the Era of Good Feelings," I found myself saying, "People were settling this region and carving out nice little farms. Some of you still live on those farms. When James Monroe became president, he wanted to raise the price of land in this area, but Congress thought settlement was more important than revenue, so they actually made it so you could buy as little as eighty acres at a time. Pretty soon, Ohio was the fourth biggest state."

"Why are we talking about James Monroe?" Cassidey asked.

"This is important," I said, immediately realizing how inadequate that was.

"Is this going to be on the AP test?" another student asked.

"I don't know," I said. "No."

So I stopped lecturing, and we took another practice AP test for the rest of the time, and I sat there wondering why I came in at all.

Cassidey lingered for a few minutes after the bell, and I tried to ignore her by packing up my bag like I was in a rush. "Are you sure you're okay?" she asked. She stretched up to wind her hair into a bun, which showed her hip bones again and a little chain dangling from her belly button.

"I'm fine," I said. "One of those days, I guess."

"I understand," she said. "I have to work until close tonight. We get pretty busy at the bar on Fridays." Cassidey worked over at the Applebee's.

"They let you serve alcohol?"

"They aren't supposed to," she said, grinning mischievously. She sat next to me on the edge of my desk. "But who's going to tell? Like, who really cares anyway? Everybody around here drinks."

Right then Hal Owens came to the door, probably to check on the substitute teacher I'd sent home. "What are you doing here?"

"That's what I said, Mr. Owens," Cassidey said.

Hal looked at her, clearly making unflattering assumptions that he wouldn't have made if she were ugly.

"Just wanted to get out of the house," I said.

Hal stood there for a beat longer. "Okay. See you later."

"Anyway," Cassidey said immediately after he'd moved on, "like I said, we get kind of busy, but there's usually room at the bar."

"Well," I said, "hang in there tonight."

She walked toward the door and pulled her bag up over her shoulder. "Oh, yeah," she said. "Could you write me a letter for Ohio State?"

"Sure," I said, thinking that she probably wouldn't get in to Ohio State and that she was almost certainly applying for the wrong reasons. Columbus ate these small town kids alive. Ohio State? Yale? For a girl like Cassidey, the difference was negligible.

I went over to Khulman's Funeral Parlor after that and tried to get a casket. Maxine Khulman, who ran the day-to-day, was someone I knew in the sense that we waved when we saw each other after Mass, but we never stopped to chat. The Khulmans were a family of long-lived people, most of them going past a hundred, which I'd always found funny in a way you couldn't say out loud. The Khulmans had always lived in town, and we had always lived outside of town, and even now that meant a gulf hung between us.

"Look," she said and pulled her reading glasses off. "I'm so sorry to hear about your father. A real tough old bird. But legally it can get messy if I sell you a casket and I know you're going to use it on land that hasn't gone through proper zoning."

"Jesus, Maxine," I said, "We've been using our plot for two-hundred years. The whole damn family is buried out there. We can't be the only people around here who still use a family plot."

"You put me in a tough position here, Ralph."

"I know," I said, trying to sound empathetic even though I was just annoyed. All the permission you need to die now. "What if I just left a check here on your desk and you happened to leave open your back door with some basic model. Plausible deniability. That's what Allen Dulles called it during the Cold War." Fifty years old, and even now when I talked to people in town, people who didn't run plow, I still felt the need to remind them I was educated. I always felt crummy after I did it, but I also couldn't stop myself.

So I wrote her a check for $1,200, knowing that the account didn't have much more than $300 in it, but that was Maxine's problem now. Her son helped me load the casket into the back of the truck, and I drove home. My brother Mark's car was parked in my usual spot. It was a low-riding Mercedes or Audi something that looked more like a spaceship than a car. I pictured him easing it down our long lane, trying to keep the gravel from kicking up into the undercarriage.

I poured us each a rye, and we sat at the kitchen table looking out over the flat white fields. It was something I could do for hours if I had the time. The farm had never stopped being beautiful to me, beautiful in a stern, austere sort of way. Mark preferred hills and golf courses. He resented our childhood in Ohio so much he moved to Indiana, which was dumb enough it made me think I could be a banker too. Every year he flew down to Myrtle Beach with some young tart he was seeing. One year, when we were still in our thirties, he'd convinced me to go along, and it took about twenty minutes to realize I didn't like golf, beaches, or Southerners.

"Well," Mark said, "what now? You think Charlie might be interested?"

He was a banker, so this was predictable. The farm was just an asset to him. "We need food and booze for the wake," I said, and he nodded.

I'd just managed to save a few hundred bucks. If I kept up like this, we might actually finance the old man's death. We sat there for a while, each drinking our ryes, trying to not breathe too loudly into the silence. We both knew we couldn't really talk anymore.

Later he said, "We could set up a lease-to-own deal with Charlie. That might make things easier."

"Until mom dies, you mean."

He poured himself another drink and set the bottle on his side of the table. "What are you going to do, live here alone? Farm alone and teach at the same time?"

"I'll figure something out," I said, already knowing that was a lie.

We had an early dinner of beef barley stew that my mother made, and then she turned in early. "I'm so glad to have you both back in this house," she said, and kissed each of us on the forehead. That was as close to affection as my mother ever got.

Mark and I had one more drink each, which meant the bottle was about empty. "How the hell do you sleep here?" Mark asked. "It's so quiet you can't fart."

I couldn't figure out why he had to say things like that. It's not like he lived in Manhattan. "I like the quiet," I said.

"Let's head into civilization and grab a drink."

We took his car, which turned out to be a Saab, just as expensive but twice as crummy as an Audi. The leather seats were freezing. Why did people like leather? Cold in winter, sticky in summer, pretentious in whatever time was left over, which wasn't much in Ohio.

We had two options, neither of them good. Friday was karaoke night at the Slow Pour, a low, concrete-blocked place that still let people smoke. The karaoke was still new. I went one time with a few other teachers. Watching a bent-over farmer in Carhartts trying to sing Hank Williams is enough to make you glad you're surrounded by so much alcohol. I didn't want to deal with any of that, so I told him the Slow Pour went out of business, and we headed over to the Applebee's.

Cassidey was leaning over the bar talking to some old guy in a button-up shirt when we walked in. She smiled at me, and I waved awkwardly.

"You came," she said and set down a couple of cocktail napkins in front of us. "And you brought your brother."

Mark and I instinctively turned and looked at each other. I guess we did still look alike. I ordered a Pabst, and Mark ordered a Dewar's and some dark beer that had chocolate and apricots in it.

"They let high school students tend bar now?" Mark asked.

I shrugged. Normally I wouldn't be caught dead drinking in front of a student, but my father was dead, and my principal already knew it, and I figured this gave me some leeway.

Cassidey came back and set our drinks in front of us. "A PBR for Ralph and a whiskey and Apricot Bock for Ralph's brother." She leaned over the bar, and her cleavage poured out of her shirt, which was just a regular t-shirt, but she had cut a long slit vertically down the neckline. Every inch of cut probably represented several dollars in extra tips. "Do you live in town, Ralph's brother?" she asked. "I don't think I've seen you before."

"I live in Fort Wayne. Just in town for the funeral."

I glared at him but didn't say anything.

"Who died?"

Mark realized he'd been an idiot then, and he looked away. For a few beats we didn't say anything until I said, "Our dad. Last night."

"Jesus," Cassidey said. "Jesus, sorry, Ralph." She turned away and poured us a couple whiskeys. "On the house," she said.

She moved away for a while then to help her other customers. She was right that it got crowded on Friday nights. I wondered how many people here were avoiding the Slow Pour like us. That bar had been in town fifty years at least. I realized then that the karaoke machine was probably their sad attempt to get people to stop coming here.

"How long have you been dropping the hammer on her?" Mark asked.

I ignored that. "She wants to go to Ohio State."

"Good for her. Get out of this place. You could learn from her."

"I like it here."

"Look," he said. "Just let me talk to Charlie. Take his temperature. We play it right, we can squeeze from either side, good cop, bad cop."

Mark shot both of his whiskeys and then sipped on his beer. We watched the commotion of the place, but mostly I think we both watched Cassidey. I should have been thinking about the farm, but when she squatted to haul up a case of beer, her thong showed, which stole my focus. After a while, as the bar started to thin out, she came back and stood by us.

"I guess that's why you were absent today, huh?"

I nodded.

"But you came back in because you just had to teach our class. You missed us. Admit it."

Normally, I would have been annoyed by the way she pivoted back to herself, which all teenagers know how to do, but there was something honest about it. She was the only person who didn't say my father was a good one or a tough old bird. "I guess we should get going," I said and fumbled for my wallet, hoping Mark would get to his faster. I don't know why I thought that. Bankers are good at reaching for your wallet but not their own. Mark got up and went to the bathroom, and I paid with all the cash I had, twenty-four dollars. I handed it to Cassidey and told her to keep it, and our forefingers grazed.

"I'm real sorry about your dad," she said and made this sad-looking smile. I believed her.

Mark and I didn't talk on the drive home, but as we were driving down Cherry Street, he saw something that made him say "This town" in a sad voice.

Mark snored through the night. I was exhausted but couldn't fall asleep. I thought about my father out there in the barn and about how what Mark said about selling was probably right but still felt wrong. That bled into thoughts about Cassidey's letter and then about her thong and hip bones. Sometimes when we aren't paying attention, grief and desire and shame mutate and become one big dirty puddle.

I got up at sunrise and went out into the cold and dug my father's grave. As the blade buried into the frozen sod, I wondered how my ancestors dug graves in winter. Shovels don't work in soil this frozen. Even a spud bar can't do much against an Ohio winter. Did they leave the body in the barn until spring thaw? Did they work around it, sometimes for months at a time, until they hardly noticed it anymore?

When I'd finished, I drove the backhoe behind the barn and siphoned out a few gallons of diesel into our tank. To hell with Charlie Garcher, I thought.

We ate breakfast in silence, the three of us. Silence is best when it exists because people are already thinking the same things. The rest of the day would consist of small talk and sad smiles and enough alcohol to keep us polite but not so much that it turned us honest.

The sad thing about a wake, at least when the departed is as old as my father, is that most of his friends are already dead. Sons and daughters pay their respects out of politeness rather than grief, and it starts to feel like a piece of well-meaning theater. Most of the people who came were from my generation, teachers and other farmers and some of the folks who ran dying little businesses in town. It reminded me a lot of my high school reunion. It wasn't long before Charlie Garcher and my brother were off in a corner, drinking and scheming. I couldn't hear their words, but I knew what they were saying.

Cassidey showed up at 5:30, out of breath and still dressed in her Applebee's getup. I was talking to Hal Owens and his wife when she walked in. Hal was telling me to take a few days' personal time, tie things up around here, buy something nice for my mother, spend one night getting too drunk. I was trying to work Cassidey's recommendation letter into the conversation in hopes of clarifying what he saw the other day. We both looked up and saw her, and Hal looked at me, probably waiting for me to make some bad explanation, but I didn't say anything, and Hal didn't push it. He would have to call me down next week and start asking uncomfortable questions, and I wasn't even sure my answers mattered. When I looked over a little later, Cassidey was in a corner, talking to my brother, and I felt a twinge of jealousy and then embarrassment. This was somehow worse than his scheming with Charlie Garcher.

Later, when I was leaving the bathroom, Charlie himself cornered me. He told me how nice the wake was, how much everyone missed my father, and I said thanks and didn't mean it even a little bit. Then he pressed a scrap of paper into my palm and walked away, and even though I didn't want to look at that offer and I hated Charlie even more for doing it right then, I couldn't help myself, and when I did, my heart just about stopped because it was such a big number. Jesus, I thought. There's no way to unsee that.

A little while later, I was walking through the barnyard to the grave, where we had a short service prepared. I was still fighting the reverie from Charlie's offer on the farm. All those zeros. Cassidey walked up next to me. "I know why you were talking about James Monroe," she said.

"How's that?"

"The Era of Good Feelings. James Monroe. You were sad about your dad dying, but you were also being ironic the way you are sometimes. Most people don't get your humor, but I do."

"How was I being ironic?"

"You know," she said, "like the way the Era of Good Feelings wasn't always so nice. The way things always seem better when we look back. Nostalgia, I guess. Plus, like how we were settling here and making farms out of the land, but how it already belonged to the Indians."

She was right about all of that. This was Shawnee territory. Whether it was my family or the Garchers running plow here, it wasn't really our land. It made me wonder if maybe she would get into Ohio State. I'd have to take her letter more seriously than I sometimes did. "Well," I said, "I'm glad you read about it."

Cassidey turned and looked around to see if anyone was in earshot. "You should come visit me next year in Columbus."

There was no ignoring that. "Well," I said, but Christ if my pants didn't tighten up, right there in the cold, walking out to bury my father. "Look. I need to go do this right now. Thanks for coming." I sped up my pace and got to the grave, and a few minutes later we were lowering the casket into the ground, and all the while I was picturing myself with Cassidey, her on top, that dangly belly chain tickling my chest. I hated myself right then. We all threw a handful of dirt on the casket, and we went back inside to finish drinking the liquor. I could wait until the morning to backfill the hole.

It was dark by the time everyone left. Mark stumbled into the back room and fell asleep on the couch there. Cassidey slipped out when I wasn't looking, which made me wonder if all her flirting was just about getting a good letter out of me, and suddenly I felt more stupid than dirty. My mother was trying to clean up, and I told her to stop, that we could get it in the morning. I fell asleep on the couch trying to think about my father but mostly thinking about Cassidey.

I woke up in the middle of the night to the sound of something scraping out by my father's grave. My brother was right about the way sound carries around here. Christ, I thought, coyotes. They're all over these parts, buzzards on land. I dressed quickly and grabbed the twelve-gauge and eased out the back door. I walked through the tracks we had all made, and I held the shotgun at a half-aim and shined a flashlight at the grave, ready to see the reflection from those yellow eyes dart away, but what I saw was my mother. She was half in the hole and seemed to be struggling to get out.

"What the hell are you doing out here, mom?"

"Come help me," she said.

I walked over and dropped the shotgun in the snow and climbed down into the hole with her. I had to straddle the casket in a way that didn't feel particularly dignified for my father or for me. "Mom. Jesus, what's going on?"

"I thought I could do it on my own."

"Do what?"

"Just help me," she said. "Stop with all the questions."

"Mom."

"Look," she said, and I could tell she was more embarrassed than frustrated. "You're smart. We sent you to college. So do the math. I'm old. This will be me soon. I don't even know how you managed to pay for this casket. How did you get this one?"

"Mom," I said, "why are you doing this now? We'll figure it out. We always do."

"I'm figuring it out right now. We're not paying for two caskets."

"Jesus," I said, though I'm not even sure the words came out. "Has it come to this?"

"Come to what?" she asked, and I realized that it had always been like this.

I stared down at my father for a minute. She had managed to pull him halfway out of the casket, but he just hung there on the edge, his back twisted awkwardly like a hose curled the wrong direction. Together we pulled him out and then hauled the casket inside the barn and set it up on the ply where my father's body had been, and that's where it would sit for a couple years until my mother died. Then we went back out to fill my father's grave in, and I told my mother to go inside, that I would take care of it.

"Look," she said, "we all still loved him."

"I know it that, Mom." I started shoveling dirt on top of my father, trying futilely to avoid his face.

She arched her back and looked up at the sky. It was overcast, no stars, brutal Ohio cold, but she looked up for a long time, probably just to avoid eye contact. "I'm so glad you came back to us after college," she said. "Your father was convinced we'd never see you again, but I told him you knew where you belonged." She didn't wait for a response. She walked back to the house, and in the morning we both pretended nothing had happened.

For the next half hour I tossed dirt into my father's grave. It almost felt good, just the two of us at the end. It made me think of the time he took me walleye fishing up in Michigan, which was a story I should have worked into his obituary. I was eleven and had never been out of Ohio. We drove up on a Saturday evening and slept in the truck bed. It was a warm, clear night, and I was on a real vacation with my father. In the morning, we stopped at a small station. "I forgot to dig for night crawlers," he said. "What will we do?" I said, worried we would have to go home, and he said, "I'll figure something out." He went inside the station for a long time. Then he came out, muttering to himself, and dug his hands into the seat cracks and the glove compartment of the truck. When he didn't find what he was looking for, he pulled his Case knife out of his pocket and looked at it longingly, and for a minute I worried he was going to do something crazy. It had been his father's knife, and one day I hoped it would be my knife, but that would never happen. He stomped back into the station, and a few minutes later, he came out with a small tub of night crawlers. Had he robbed them? I wondered until we reached the shoreline, but the water of Lake Erie was so green and beautiful, so immense, that I soon stopped thinking about it.

We sat at the edge of a long concrete pier, and we fished together. The sun was nice, and the breeze was nice, and I had the whole day with my father. I caught four fish, two bluegills, a walleye, and a perch. We cleaned the walleye and the perch and tossed back the bluegills. My father didn't catch anything at all, which was a point of pride for me. He was fishing a naked hook, of course, but I didn't know that then, just like I didn't know he'd traded away his knife. By the time we ran out of a bait, it was getting dark, and we needed to drive home. I'd been trolling the bottom with a treble hook for the last hour or so, and I realized I'd gotten hung up. We switched poles so my father could try to get mine free. He yanked and twisted, pulled on the line, but it wouldn't come free.

I reeled his line in and saw that his hook was cleaned.

"Guess they got me again," he said.

"Sorry, dad," I said. "I guess we'll just have to cut mine."

He reached into his pocket for his knife and realized it wasn't there. Then he just yanked at my line as hard as he could, which ripped the leader clean off. He tousled my hair and we threw the poles in the truck bed and drove home, where I bragged to my mother and brother about how I'd caught fish but my father hadn't. I was eleven years old. I had no idea that my father was the world's quietest hero.

I finished filling in the grave and tamped down the loose soil and squatted next to him. There was no headstone, not for my father, not for anyone else, but I knew who was where.

How to Throw a Punch

There's a guy who works down the line from you, Mick Sligo, and he's convinced you stole the king of spades from his deck of cards. He plays euchre during breaks, and he needs that king of spades. He pokes you in the chest, hard, says you need to give it back pronto. He's a brutish sort of guy, tattooed forearms, shaved head, mound of beer gut. He wears cut-off shirts and always manages to sweat through them until they look translucent with grease. He drives a Chevy with six wheels and tells loud jokes about Polacks.

You did not steal Mick Sligo's king of spades, but that hardly seems to matter. You try to reason with him. What would you do with a single king of spades? It's an odd thing to steal, no? Mick Sligo doesn't care. His blood is up, and he's chosen you. Find it by the end of the shift, he says. He does not say *or else*, does not explain what he will do to you when you do not find it.

You realize that for first time in your life, you'll need to throw a punch. Mick Sligo cannot be reasoned with. He's a hulking barbarian, and you can hardly blame him for choosing combat over diplomacy. You think of your wife and three-year-old daughter at home, asleep. You moved to second shift when she was born so you could see them during the day. But you ended up on the same team as Mick Sligo. Your wife won't approve of violence, but she'll help ice you down when you get home, hopefully your knuckles, but probably your jaw.

You need to know that this probably won't end well. You shouldn't punch guys who have lots of tattoos. You shouldn't punch guys who are more than a head taller than you or a foot wider than you. You shouldn't punch guys who seem too eager. You shouldn't punch guys with fighter nicknames: Snake, T-Rex, Bomber, Ninja, Mick Sligo.

If you have any say, it's better to punch guys who wear things like this: bow ties, braces, top hats, eye patches, prosthetic arms. Punch guys who have lots of facial piercings. Punch guys who've just eaten a big burrito. Punch guys with chronic diarrhea.

But in your case, the fight seems inevitable. You'll have to punch Mick Sligo. You should know that you'll look ridiculous throwing a punch at first. Everyone does. You'll swing too hard, end up falling on your can. You'll tweak your wrist. You'll miss by two feet. Think of the time when you were sixteen at the turnabout dance, and Marla Wolters let you take her bra off one-handed; it will be that awkward.

So you need to practice before the fight. Head to the bathroom during every line stop. Go into the handicapped stall. Start by spreading your legs to shoulder width. Then scissor them so they're catty-cornered, left in front of right. This distributes your weight the right way to keep you from falling on your can. Practice bouncing your weight from your back leg to your front leg. That's where your power comes from. You see lots of those schmucks with muscles growing all over their arms and necks like tumors, jerks who swing with only their shoulders. These guys are idiots. Never took a physics class. Real power comes from your hips and your legs. It's technique, all of it. Practice swinging like this: Two jabs and an uppercut. Two jabs and an overhand right. Two jabs and anything. Those jabs set everything else up. They don't need to connect; they just need to change his posture. And when they do, you flatten him.

You want your knuckles to connect, not the hairy part of your fingers. That's a good way to dislocate a finger. Keep your wrists locked tight. Don't bend them at all or they'll crumple. Punch into the meat of your hand for practice. Your knuckles should go deep into it. It should start to bruise. Do this over and over. Let Mick Sligo see you do this. Do not make eye contact with him all night. Do not look at him when his back is to you. He could turn around at any moment. Focus on what you must do, which is punch Mick Sligo hard enough that he's convinced you did not steal his king of spades.

When the moment comes, do not partake in pre-fight antics. Do not tell Mick Sligo, "Bitch, I'm gonna to drop you like a B-52." Do not bump chests. Do not say mama jokes. Walk directly up to Mick Sligo, scissor your legs, torque your hips, and pop him in the temple.

This is the most important rule of throwing a punch: always get the first punch in. Street fighting is not pugilism; it's a race. Most people have never been hit in the head. It rattles your damn bones. The earth tilts on its axis and goes fuzzy. You feel incapable of basic thought. Scientists did a study and found that even twenty minutes after head trauma, subjects could not do basic long division or identify secondary colors (fuchsia, magenta, puce). You must do this to Mick Sligo. Even if he recovers, you got that one punch in, and that's something. Make him forget puce.

At the end of the shift, Mick Sligo will look down the line at you. His cut-off will be translucent, his chest hair underneath clinging to it like tiny, fibrous worms. You will feel his eyes on you for several moments before you decide to look up and meet them. When you do, they will look mean and hungry, as if you are the porterhouse that he is rearing to eat. But you will stare straight back. Perhaps you will even nod at him. Perhaps you are feeling particularly roguish, and you wink. Perhaps you hope to be remembered for a dash of bravado, which is a perfectly natural wish.

Regardless, you will eventually turn away, grab your cooler, and head toward the exit. You will feel a commotion behind you, a growing crowd of interest. You will feel Mick Sligo back there also. It is a long walk, back upstairs, across the bridge that spans the line, past the air-conditioned sales offices. You will stop to clock out, and you will feel the crowd growing, growing closer to you. You will fumble with your ID and be forced to rescan it twice. You will taste something sharp and metallic, and this will be the adrenaline. Your torso will grow cold with fear.

"Hey!"

You'll hear it behind you, not far. The unmistakable yell of Mick Sligo seeking his king of spades. But you will not turn around. You will move forward, past the security desk, through the foyer, and out into the parking lot. The night air will splash your face like cold water, and you will breathe it deeply as if surfacing. The crowd of men, twenty or so, instinctively circles around you.

And then the hand on your shoulder, twisting you around. You know it's the meaty paw of Mick Sligo. You know what you must do. As he spins you around, you twist into position, left in front of right, scissored, and by the time you're face to face with the lumbering Neanderthal, you're already into your swing. The world slows for that first punch. You must enjoy this because everything seems to speed up from there. But for now, it blurs, and you are swinging, torquing your hips into him, and your middle knuckle connects square with Mick Sligo's temple. He drops into a heap. Just instantly drops. There is no pause, no wail of pain, no wobbles like a Jenga tower. You punch, he drops. He does not move. He lies there like an oversized trash bag full of yard waste.

For a moment, all will go quiet. The crowd will stare at Mick Sligo, wondering if he will get up and take his revenge on you. It was not supposed to happen this way, even you know this, and the onlookers seem confused. But Mick Sligo does not get up.

You'll probably want to stand over him at this point, spread your legs, and puff your chest like a marauding Spartan. You've certainly earned the right. But you should also know that such an action is perhaps the start of something else entirely. This is the last thing you need to know about throwing a punch: it's addictive. Once you learn how to do it, you want to do it often. The desire to throw a punch will soon overtake its rare necessity. You feel it already, don't you? You'll feel it from now on, during every conversation, like a pistol burning to be loosed from its holster.

Unicorn Stew

Bev and me, we're cooking up some unicorn stew in a trash can and punching each other. We have a sign and everything, silver spray paint on plywood, so any other craphead kids know what we're doing. *Do Not Disturb!* it says, *Making Unicorn Stew.* It's boiling hot outside, and we don't want to deal with their interruptions and stupid questions, like, "Did you know that my dad killed a bigger unicorn than you did?" or "Did you use a regular gun or a plasma laser to kill the unicorn?" or "You should have made unicorn ice cream," which isn't even a question at all.

The stew has other things in it besides unicorns. Like potatoes, because without potatoes it'd be soup, not stew. Also Fruit Roll-Ups and tartar sauce because it does need some seasoning. Bev steals all of it from the store, and we have to tell her dad that right away, so he knows we didn't spend any of his money. He's already pretty sore about me staying with them while my dad is out driving his truck. He glares at me during dinner, and all I can do is stare at his big brown mustache and think about how tough it makes him look. He says I eat too much, but I always make sure to eat a little less than Bev does. "We don't have money for you little piss-heads to be wasting it on your dumb piss-head games," he'll say about our unicorn stew. But then Bev will promise him that we didn't pay for anything. We boosted it all from the packie.

The problem is that Bev's dad doesn't usually believe people, so he might still get rough. He might still thwack our knees with the little flashlight he carries on his belt.

We drop in the ingredients, and then we punch each other. "Potato incoming!" I shout and then sock her in the shoulder. Lemon-Lime Kool-Aid incoming! she shouts and hits me in the thigh. Pepperoni log!—punch. Creamed corn!—punch. We go on like this for a long time until the trash can is pretty full. We keep adding water from the garden hose. It's so hot out we're both sweating like crazy people. It's that wet sort of heat, the kind that makes it hard to breathe. I want to peel my sweaty shirt off, but I don't because Bev has to keep hers on, Bev being a girl.

The reason we punch each other is to make bruises. Bev gets them from her dad, who doesn't like cigarette smoke or C-minuses for spelling "besiege" wrong. He mostly leaves me alone, but I get my bruises from seventh-graders, soccer players with shaggy bowl cuts, who wait for me in the little hallway by the cafeteria and don't think I should have red hair or pigeon-toes unless I want to be a major league faggot. Bev and me are only in the fifth grade, and we can't do much about it. So we make new bruises on each other, and they mix in with the old ones, and then we don't know where any of them came from. Bev's a head taller than I am, like most of the girls in our grade, and she hits hard, but I don't admit this or complain about her sharp knuckle punches because I'm the one getting the better bruises, after all.

Bev's mom is sitting in her broken car, on the street, smoking and listening to the Sox game. I think she's watching over us too. It has to be about a million degrees inside that car, but there she is. Bev's dad won't have smoke in the house since he says he wants to quit, and what Bev's dad says goes. He works across the river at the Necco Wafer factory and always smells extra sweet, like he maybe has a bunch of cotton candy in his pockets. Sometimes he'll bring home a sack of little heart-shaped candies, the ones rich kids put in Valentine's Day cards. But he has the crummy, messed up ones with mistakes in the lettering where the machine marked them all wrong or off-center or something. I guess they can't sell those, so he steals some and brings them home. Most say dumb crap. Don't even look like real words. Some are kind of close—*Luove yo, Cute tie, So Buel!* You have to use your imagination. My favorite was one that was probably supposed to say *Love Bird* but ended up all mashed and crooked, so it looked kind of like *Lve Tird.* Bev likes the one we found last year. We think it was supposed to be two different hearts that said *Be Good* and *Lover Boy*, but they got blended somehow and so it sort of looks like *God Lover!*

Mostly, though, we just eat the little candies up until our stomachs are all bloated, like we drank way too much root beer. Then we shoot the rest at each other with slingshots and call each other love turd and God-lover. Little heart bullets, and boy, do they leave marks.

So Bev's mom sits in the car and smokes and listens to the Sox game, even though it's hot enough to make your face melt off. And the Sox are almost definitely losing again. We can hear that grumbly radio voice echo every time the other team knocks a hit. Sometimes she looks over at us and shakes her head, probably thinking that we should be making broccoli casserole instead of unicorn stew.

Walter Sullivan rides by on his ten-speed. He lives two streets over in a first floor place with a yard. It's a new house. There was this humongous fire here a few years ago, destroyed all kinds of crap. People like Walter Sullivan got new houses out of it. But a lot of other people just moved away from Chelsea. I don't blame them for that. Our house was mostly okay, but a couple blocks away—total burnout. Still lots of houses people haven't really rebuilt on or even cleaned up too good. All this charcoaled crap in big heaps, and I guess no one really has money to do anything about. So Bev and me like to scrounge around and find cool junk that didn't burn, like huge bolts and spigots that we can pretend are guns. We paint charcoal mustaches on each other, try to get them as big as we can. Then we scowl and shoot at each other and try to die in the most convincing sort of way. Sometimes we just sit on the curb with our mustaches and act angry about adult stuff, like taxes and cigarettes and indigestion.

Walter Sullivan stares at our unicorn stew sign. He got popular last year because his parents got divorced, and his dad started buying him lots of great stuff, like ten-speeds and kites and gummy worms. Sometimes, when it's really hot, Bev and me will go over Walter's house and do his big sprinkler, but mostly we don't. Mostly we like to be on our own.

Walter stares at our sign, and he gets this look on his face like he's trying to do long division homework. "Where's the horn?" he asks, and I tell him it's already in there, cooking, and that he's a dummy who smells like armpit fungus. Everyone knows you put the horn in first because it gives everything more flavor.

"God-lover," Bev says, and she belts him in the arm.

Walter stands there, straddling his ten-speed and rubbing his arm. "I don't get it," he says.

Bev yanks him off his ten-speed and puts him into a headlock and starts cranking. She does it fast, like she was looking for a reason to go after Walter. And while she's holding him, I ball up my fist and noogie him till my knuckles burn. It's a big problem, the way some kids act when their dumb divorced parents start buying them expensive crap.

Bev lets go, and Walter tries to fix his hair and stand up straight like maybe we were just palling around on him.

"You should probably stir it some," he says.

Bev and me look at each other. We haven't thought of this, and even though we should bash Walter's shoulder, we don't because he's probably right.

"If you have a big spoon," Bev says, "I guess we could let you help out."

So Walter pedals away toward his house. As he's turning the corner, Bev shouts at him to bring some of those gummy worms too.

We stare down at our pot of unicorn stew. We're out of ingredients to drop in, so we start in on handfuls of crabgrass and dandelion heads and thistles.

Someone gets a hit, probably the other team, and the radio voice jumps loud for a minute. Bev's mom isn't smoking anymore, but she's still sitting in the car. She looks over at us with this sort of sad, drooping face, like maybe she just woke up. Bev waves at her and then says, "My mom's a dumbo. I'd smoke in the house if I wanted to."

I don't say anything, but I also don't believe her. Her dad scares me. He's awfully big, way bigger than my dad, and even though he smells like cotton candy, he's mean. He's always calling Bev's mom a shit-cow and shouting at Bev to run down to the packie for him. When he drives away in his big blue truck, he always squeals the tires. One time after he elbowed Bev's mom in the face, he got all serious, saying how sorry he was, and why did she make him do ugly things like that to prove how much he loved her and how much it made his heart hurt? Another time Bev stayed home from school for a whole week because she said she had bronchitis. Her dad wouldn't even let me in our room to see her. I'm pretty sure she didn't really have bronchitis, though, because I stood outside the door and never heard any coughing. And when I finally got in to see her, she had this mashed up pinky toe. What I think happened was her dad was working on the big blue truck, and Bev asked him some question, and I guess it was the wrong question because he dropped one of his hammers on her toe, which broke it hard. I'm not saying he hit her with it, but her toe was in bad shape. Even now it hasn't really healed, just seems like bone dust wrapped in skin, like a sugar packet, maybe. So Bev always wears her mom's old sneakers tied double-tight.

Our dads used to be pals. They both worked at the candy plant and liked to come home and sit on the curb and toss rocks into the sewer grate. Then when it rained the water didn't drain right, and Bev and me could jump around in this huge, muddy puddle. Sometimes we'd tie yarn to sticks and pretend to fish in it. They were both a little nicer then, I think because having a friend makes you nicer. But then my dad decided to become a trucker and Bev's dad didn't, so they aren't really friends anymore. Now Bev's dad is meaner. My dad comes back for a weekend every couple months, and he takes me to Dairy Queen and the movie theater, but then he drops me back off at Bev's house and doesn't come inside. He says he likes to sleep in his truck now. Bev's dad never comes out to talk to him. Bev thinks my dad just wanted to leave Chelsea, and maybe she's right. She says that one time when he's back, we should be real nice to him at first. Wait till he's sleeping in his truck and then do something really bad, like hit him with a baseball bat or dump a bucket of puke on his head. But I don't think I could do that.

Walter Sullivan comes back, pedaling extra hard. He hands Bev an oar that he stole from his dad's canoe. Bev looks at me and shrugs. "The gummy worms?" she says.

Walter reaches into his pocket and pulls out a fresh pack and starts opening it.

"We'll do the ingredients," Bev says and grabs them up.

Then we start stirring it with the oar and dropping in gummy worms. So the rule becomes this: every tenth circle around the pot, you get punched because we do still need to keep making these bruises even if we are pretty fantastic chefs.

But Walter doesn't like this. Bev bashes his shoulder, and he starts to tear up. None of the other kids ever hit Walter Sullivan because then they won't get to play with his toys.

"I don't want to stir anymore," Walter says.

"You don't stir, you have to leave," Bev says.

Walter reaches for the canoe paddle, but Bev steps in front of him. "We'll bring it back to you when we're done," she says.

Then he squats down for his bike, but Bev stomps on the front tire. "We need to borrow this too," Bev says.

Walter looks over at me, like he's hoping I'll help him out, but I don't say anything. "Come on, guys," he says and pulls on the handlebars a little harder.

Bev just shakes her head at him.

By now Walter Sullivan is crying and yelling something about sending his dad down here just as soon as he gets home from work. Then he just runs off without his bike.

I keep stirring the unicorn stew while Bev rides Walter's bike around. She does all kinds of wheelies and jumps off the curb. Then she starts going all the way to the end of the street and turning around, pedaling as fast as she can, and by the time she gets back, she's flying. Then she jams on the brakes and turns sideways and skids out. It leaves these long black marks in the road, and every time she does it, she makes one a little bit longer. Then it's my turn to make the skid marks. It feels good to ride fast because it's like wind, but I can't seem to skid out as good as Bev. She has longer legs and goes faster, I guess. So I go back to our unicorn stew and leave the bike riding to her.

Bev's mom is still in the car, still listening to the Sox. She watches us riding Walter Sullivan's bike, but she doesn't get out and say anything. It's almost five o'clock, which means Bev's dad is coming home soon, and after working all day in the candy plant, he's pretty grumpy, and he's liable to call people shit-cows or mash their toes up if his boss was an extra big jerk today, which he usually is.

At twelve minutes after five the big blue truck rumbles way down at the other end of the street. Bev drops Walter's bike and faces the opposite way, like maybe if she doesn't look, he doesn't exist. He doesn't stop all the way at the intersection, and then he guns it, and the big blue truck sounds like a space rocket or maybe Godzilla.

He squeals the tires when he stops and gets out of the big blue truck and hikes his pants up. I can tell that his boss was a jerk today. We stop stirring the unicorn stew and stand there extra quiet. He spits into the street and arches his back. Then he hears the radio and looks over toward Bev's mom in the car, and he stomps over there and heaves the door open, and this tornado of smoke pours out, and the Sox game gets louder. He swipes his hand in front of his face and leans back.

"Fucking Christ!" he says, and Bev's mom jumps over into the passenger seat.

"Inside!" he yells at her, which doesn't seem quite fair to me because I thought the deal was that she just couldn't smoke in the house. But that's just like Bev's dad—always making a deal and then breaking it.

He moves over to the passenger side of the car, and Bev's mom jumps back to the driver's seat. They go on like this for a few times, and it's kind of funny to see Bev's dad look like the dumb craphead he is, but it's also kind of not funny because once he gets a hold of her, he's liable to punch her in the neck until she cries. Pretty soon he gets tired of chasing her, so he just stands there in front of the car and spreads his legs wide like some bandit in the Wild West. Then he looks over at us for the first time. He looks at us, and then he looks at Bev's mom, and then he looks back at us.

Bev's mom gets out of the car and walks out into the street and stands kind of in between us and Bev's dad. She probably doesn't want him ruining our unicorn stew after seeing all the work we've put in to getting it just right. Bev's dad leans into the car and grabs the pack of cigarettes and lights one for himself.

"You," he says to me. "Bev's little boyfriend. Head down to the packie and get me a grinder and some Blatz. We need to have a family meeting." He hands me a wad of bills and shoves me toward the store.

The radio is still going, and I can hear it pretty clear with the doors wide open. He looks into our pot of unicorn stew and cracks his fat knuckles. "What's all this shit?"

"We're making unicorn stew," Bev says, and I think she speaks up just so she can look tough in front of me, but it's a risky thing to do, talking to Bev's dad when he's upset.

"Bev's little boyfriend," he says to me, "go to the packie."

Then he turns to Bev. "Time to come inside," he says. He takes one last puff of his cigarette and tosses it right into our pot of unicorn stew. Then he crumples up the rest of the pack and throws that in there, too, and that rubs me hard because you don't get to just ruin other people's unicorn stew.

Bev looks over at me. She has this sad face on, like her mom's, but I really don't know what to do. Everybody says you need to stand up for yourself, but they forget that when you're in the fifth grade, most people are bigger than you. And I have to sleep somewhere. So I just stand there. Bev hands me the oar and walks inside without saying goodbye or anything. And as soon as Bev leaves, so does her mom. Then it's just me and Bev's dad, which is not the kind of situation you want to get yourself into if you like your toes.

"Where'd all this come from?" he says, meaning our unicorn stew.

I was counting on Bev doing the talking because I'm not very good at talking to her dad. "We didn't pay for anything," I say.

And he glares at me with his mean glare, the kind where his lips sort of curl in around his teeth and make his mustache stand out even more. It probably didn't matter what I said.

"That was Bev's idea, eh?" he says, and I don't exactly nod, but I don't say no either, and so he knows everything, I guess.

He turns to go inside, but right then Walter Sullivan and his dad come around the corner. Walter's dad works at the candy plant, too, so I guess it didn't take Walter long to tell on us. His dad looks mad, but I think if we had some kind of contest to see who could be the meanest or the maddest, Bev's dad would beat just about anybody no problem.

"That's my kid's bike," Walter's dad says. He's tall and skinny and has this huge nose. He looks a little like the Fruit Loops bird, except for he isn't blue.

Bev's dad looks down at me. "He let Bev borrow it," I say, which is definitely what Bev would say.

"My kid says he was just borrowing it," Bev's dad says.

"Your kid's lying."

Bev's dad takes a step forward, so he's right in front of Walter's dad. And when he does that, I follow him, take a step toward Walter. They don't move, like they don't really know what to do. "My kids don't lie," Bev's dad says.

"Look, Jake," Walter's dad says, "Either way, it's my kid's bike, and he wants it back now."

"Sure," says Bev's dad. But then he doesn't step aside. "Just apologize to my kid for saying he's a liar."

Walter's dad gives him this awful look, like he's trying to eat a handful of gravel. And the way Walter stares at his dad makes me feel pretty awful. I don't know why Bev's dad always has to get the push on people, but he does.

For a minute nobody moves. Then Walter's dad squats down in front of me, just about eye level, and looks right at my face. "I'm sorry I called you a liar, pal. I shouldn't have done that."

Then he stands up, glares at Bev's dad again, and they're gone. We watch them for a minute, Walter riding on the bike while his dad walks just behind.

"And that's how you deal with a bully," Bev's dad says. He musses up my hair, which kind of hurts because his hands have these sharp calluses that scrape on my skull. But I just let him do it anyway. Then he goes inside, and I rub my head and think on the way he stood up for me and called me his kid. I start walking down to the packie with the money he forgot to take back to get some stew ingredients for tomorrow. That way Bev and me can get an early start. I pull my t-shirt out like a pouch and fill it with packs of Necco Wafers since they're the cheapest thing around, and the whole time I'm thinking about how I'm glad to be gone right now because Bev's dad still has about a zillion things to be mad about. I take our candy up to pay and dump it on the counter and unwad the dollar bills, and that's when I see the rainbow sherbet behind the ice cream counter. It's in this big, frosty bucket. I know I shouldn't put back any of our stew ingredients, I know we'll need them, but I can't help it. It's so hot out. I put back half the candy, and I stand in front of the counter and point to the rainbow sherbet and the guy fills me up a big cone. I walk toward Bev's house, and it starts dripping in the heat, sliding all down my arms, all the way to my armpits. I can feel it sticking to my face and drying like syrup. I'm in no rush to get back, I keep licking around the edges of the cone where it's all melted, but I can't keep up with the heat, and before long my shirt is lined with all these bright-colored stains that will be impossible to hide.

Stones We Throw

At Mother's wake, I threw stones at the sky. It was dark, deep snow trenches wrapping around everything like an acoustic damper. Even the hollow wail of coyote flattened into a muffled echo. I threw stones, chucking them high into the darkness, where they seemed to lodge, like stars that had forgotten how to glow or perhaps young stars that hadn't yet learned.

I hid outside in the dark while all those aunts and uncles, scary strangers, roamed our hallways and ate potato salad and made sad faces at Father, like apologies. I threw stones until my shoulder ached and thought about how I kind of liked the pain right then, like it was helping somehow.

"Come say goodbye now," Father said later, leaning out the back door.

"I want to stay out here," I said.

He hesitated on the back steps. He hadn't put a jacket on. "Caleb," he said.

"It's scary in there," I said.

He let the door close behind him and sat next to me. We were both of us out of the light that spilled from the door, but if you looked long enough, you could probably see our breath. "It is scary," he said. "I'd hoped you might save me by coming back in."

"Sorry." I wasn't, though. I was glad to be outside, away from all that, glad to have him sitting next to me, not quite touching but almost, like I could feel his heat. I rubbed on my shoulder.

"What did you do there?"

"Throwing rocks," I said.

"Not into the garden, I hope."

I shrugged. I didn't want to tell him that, yes, I'd thrown them toward the garden, but then the sky had sucked them up. They were stars now. "It hurts but kind of feels good," I said. "You know?"

"I do," he said. Then he moved over the last bit, and our hips were touching as we sat there. He unlaced his boots and took off his socks and plunged his feet into the snow all the way up past the ankle. I stared up at his face, but he wasn't looking at me. He was looking at the sky where I'd been throwing stones.

I asked then, didn't that hurt? and he said yes, some, but it also felt kind of good. We sat there like that for a long time. He never did go back inside or make me go either. When people started leaving, he didn't get up to say goodbye, just waved without turning around, his feet stuck in the snow, which seemed to confuse everyone.

I went back to school soon, and he went back to prepping for spring wheat. Everything was quieter. The house smelled strange, less lived in. Everyone kept telling us how it was still raw now, wasn't it? But it would get better. We couldn't believe how much better it would get by spring, but when thaw finally came and father ran the turnwrest through the garden, he wrecked his blade on all those stones out there, which I know he saw, but he still did it anyway, and everyone seemed to think it was an accident even though I don't think it was.

In the Walls

Frank and me, we can hang some goddamn drywall. Cut, lift, push screws. Repeat. Frank can eyeball-measure to within a quarter inch, and I can drive six screws before you clear your throat. I know the guys who come in and mud the joints get all the credit, everybody nowadays thinks drywall mudders are artists, and maybe they are the way the good ones could hide a damn hematoma with joint compound. Drywall mudders get the credit for making it all pretty, for hiding the mistakes, but Frank and me, we make the walls.

But then Frank gets canned. Our boss, Stanley, accuses him of stealing something he didn't steal, which happens more than you'd think. It's kind of like code for *We found some Mexicans to do your job*.

Stanley, who's actually just our real boss's kid, asks me, Do I know anything about a missing pneumatic hammer?

I tell him, No, I don't anything about that, which I don't.

Then he says to me, Hey, by the way, do you know where Frank's keys are? I need to move his truck because he parked me in.

I point him over to Frank's lunch cooler, not thinking much about it. But then at the end of the day, Stanley calls Frank outside and points into his truck and asks him, Hey, Frank, how did this pneumatic hammer get in your truck? You stealing from us, then, Frank? Then he shit-cans Frank, and I feel like a huge dumb idiot.

Frank doesn't make a scene or anything, I think because he's just so damn confused. He's young, never gotten fired before. He goes real calm, real deliberate in his movements, and all I can think is that's how crazy bad guys in the movies always act before they stab somebody in the dick with a samurai sword. But Frank just says, Okay, right, and leaves, and we all go back to work.

So later that night, Frank comes over, and we start drinking some, and before long, we head back to the site. It's this giant castle in the burbs with a three-car garage and travertine tiles all over. Everything's stainless steel or granite or Zapatero hardwood floors reclaimed from the Panama Canal. It's dark when we get there, we can't see much with flashlights in our mouths, but we don't want to draw attention.

Frank pulls out a cordless Makita with this tiny, 1/16-inch bit and chucks it tight. Then he goes around to all air compressors, popping these holes in the undersides of the tanks. No one will ever see them, but they'll get pissed something fierce when their tanks don't carry any pressure.

Then he squats in a bare stud wall, unbuckles his coveralls, perches there, and boy does he push. His face turns this hot red while he grimaces, and then he grunts like he's trying to bench-press a double-wide, and then there's the plop, and damn hell, it just clogs my nose up with crap-stink. I can't get away from it. Come on, he says, meaning we need to hurry up and hang some drywall around it to lock in the stink and keep anybody from finding it. Which we do.

Then it's on to the joint compound, the five-gallon tubs, jerking off into it. He's drunk and cackling now. He puts a mixer bit into the drill and churns the whole bucket up. Look, he says. You can't tell where Frank-juice stops and the mud starts! And he thinks this is just the funniest thing ever, that these yuppies are going to have a house with so much Frank in the walls. Doesn't matter how many walls we put up, they aren't getting rid of Frank.

At some point I almost tell Frank how it was kind of my fault, that I didn't mean it, but I'm still awful sorry. I don't say anything though because it won't change this whole shitpile of a situation. Doesn't matter how or why that shitpile gets in your house, you just have to deal with it. I'm older, I got replaced twice last year, but Frank hasn't. He's a young kid, likes to drink light beer and think about those girls he went to high school with but never got to see naked. It's a crummy feeling, getting canned, and all you can think of for the first couple days is how to get even. But work always turns up for guys like us. People are always going to want walls in their houses.

Frank starts hauling the double sheets of drywall then, four-by-eight sheets, out to his truck. Come on, he says. So I start helping him load them even though I don't really want to. It means tomorrow, when I go to work, I'll have to answer some questions. But I can just blame everything on teenagers, which is what you're supposed to do in my business when something goes missing.

We steal a dozen sheets and drive away, and Frank is feeling pretty great, some from the beer but some from all the getting even. A sheet of drywall only costs about four bucks, but right now they feel more valuable. Frank laughs to himself the whole ride home like we just stole the Mona Lisa or something.

When we get back to my place, Frank wants to unload it all there. I don't have the space, he says, which is true. He lives in an apartment about the size of a paper sack. So we stack them all in my TV room. We have one more beer and sit on the couch looking at them, not really saying much.

I wonder how Stanley got in my truck, Frank says then.

I feel myself clench up, but I don't say anything.

You have any idea?

I shake my head, no, and take a big drink of my beer.

Well, Frank says and then doesn't finish whatever he wanted to say. He gets up and stumbles toward the door. Guess I'll see you tomorrow, he says and leaves. Thing is, though, I won't see him tomorrow.

I flip on the TV and have one last beer, but I can't see the left side of the tube because the drywall is blocking it. There's this guy yelling at somebody, and I think it's probably his wife, but I can't be sure. He's just going nutso on her, calling her whore and skank. He's unloading, calling her shit-brain and twat. But then she starts yelling back, and it's the weirdest thing. It's like the drywall is talking. It's a woman's voice, but all I see is drywall. She calls him a liar and a dirty cheat and a bunch of other mean stuff. It's pretty annoying the way the drywall blocks her face, but I just close my eyes and figure to hell with it. I'll move it in the morning.

The next day I have three new Mexicans that I have to start training on how to hang drywall fast and proper. One of them's named Jesus and the other two aren't. They catch on quick and don't ask stupid questions, but they don't say jokes the way Frank did. Later in the day, the boss's kid pulls me aside and asks, Didn't we have more drywall than this? And what's with that weird crap smell? But this time I play dumb. Probably some no-good teenagers, I tell him.

Out of the Bronx

We hunted the rats because we were so poor.

Years later and I can still see them bolting out from that dumpster at the end of the alley, dozens of rats, squealing and scurrying. They're on fire. Roman and I are watching from the fire escape four stories up, these burning rats darting all over the place and yelping. "Burn harder, you rat-fucks!" Roman screams. He has this deranged look in his eyes, like a boxer who just got knocked out and is coming to. It's dark out, so it's almost pretty, all these burning rats scampering in every direction, like a meteor shower in the alley, and I almost say so but I decide not to. Instead, we just watch, open-mouthed, two young kids in awe of this cosmic power we've just unleashed.

The rats came from this pub on the garden level, which our landlord owned. We called him Old Irish because he had this thick brogue which sounded like a different language. Dad said that his skin was so pale it smelled like potatoes. That was Dad's one joke, which he told whenever Old Irish knocked on the door and said he had to raise the rent again. His pub served a Guinness and black pudding breakfast, that's it, and Old Irish made it all on site every morning, and so every afternoon, right before he closed up the kitchen, he tossed out a trash bag full of leftovers into the alley, a mixture of congealed blood, torn casings, and suet drippings, which is like Oreo cheesecake for rats. Old Irish didn't live in the building, so it wasn't his rat problem.

Dad threatened to call the health inspector one time after Roman woke up in the middle of the night with a rat gnawing at a scab on his knee. Old Irish stepped close, pointed a fat finger in Dad's face. "You're so cheesed about rats, maybe you should move to Brooklyn with the fancies." Dad got real quiet and just walked away. Mom was already sick then, never even got out of bed anymore and always had that hollow-eyed look, like a porcelain doll. Dad couldn't risk eviction, and Old Irish knew it.

He made his tenants rent everything: the refrigerator, the kitchen table, light bulbs, the plunger. We couldn't afford to buy our own, but we couldn't do without. Old Irish knew exactly how to get people on the hook, and he knew how to keep them there, flopping around in the shallows. "It's not like he was always rich," Dad told me one time. "I don't know why he has to treat us like that." Dad was a kind little man, and the thing about being kind is that if you don't surround yourself with other kind people, you get exploited constantly. I think on it now, and I can't imagine the humiliation Dad must have suffered, negotiating a ten-minute rental of a toilet augur, all because he had two young boys who ate too many grape-jellied meatballs at the school picnic.

For the longest time, Mom had worked first whistle and Dad worked second, which meant one of them was always gone, and one of them was always asleep. Which meant Roman and I did whatever we wanted with the understanding that we didn't have any money for bail or hospitals. But then Mom got depressed all of a sudden and wouldn't leave the apartment, so Dad started covering her shifts too. His boss told him that maybe Roman or I could slide into the job when we turned sixteen if Dad worked it for a quarter rate until then. Dad was one of those guys you'd see on the train wearing a dirty white jumpsuit, elbows on knees, not making eye contact with anyone, just bushed out because of the way his life ended up.

All of this made us easy prey, which turned me quiet and submissive like Dad. But it made Roman mean. He wanted to get even. He stole bikes from the Catholic school up the street and rode them straight down to the East River, jumping off at the last second and letting them glide on into the water without a sound. He picked fights before the other kids even had a chance to hassle him, always aiming for the nose because, he said, he liked to see rich kids cry. Some kids are poor but don't ever know it because everyone else is poor too. We knew. Bottom of the food chain poor, and the way the food chain works is there's a pecking order, you can hunt anything below you, and the only thing below us was the rats.

Jesus, the rats. They were everywhere, always just eating and chirruping their little mating calls, mating constantly, quick and violent, always making more rats like it was the most ruthless sort of addiction imaginable. It all had something to do with the way the sewers had been dug out, too shallow, lots of sewage that wouldn't fully drain, and it attracted rats. Rumor was that for every human in the South Bronx, there were two rats. You'd think we were safe because we lived up on the fourth floor, but we weren't. They climbed up through the walls, especially when it got cold out. You could hear them at night, clawing at the plaster and chirruping. We set traps, killing one or two at a time, which was like shooting a tank with a pellet gun. What we needed was needed more firepower, a full-out rat jihad.

Then one Friday afternoon, Roman showed up with a canister of potassium permanganate and a jug of antifreeze.

"What the hell?" I asked.

"Motherfucking napalm," he said.

"Bullshit. Where'd you get all that?"

Turns out potassium permanganate is just a chemical people use to clean out wells and cisterns. Mix it with antifreeze and you've got trouble. As he explained it, I remembered Roman's uncharacteristic interest in a lesson at school. It was about the moon landing, how NASA engineers developed this hypergolic engine that mixed two chemicals, and poof, the engine lit right there in the middle of space. No oxygen necessary.

"What if someone happened to mix both chemicals?" Roman had asked. "You know, just for yucks."

"I imagine it would be very bad, Roman," our teacher said.

"Fuckin'-A, it would," Roman said and grinned that mischievous hyena grin of his. He could already see it.

We sat on the fire escape all afternoon, looking down at the back door of Old Irish's pub, waiting for him to toss out the sausage slop. Roman got this calm look on his face, like he was in a trance, like you hear about guys getting just after some jungle firefight.

"So how will we—" I started to ask, but Roman cut me off.

"It'll work," he said. "It's science."

Truth is, the antifreeze probably would have killed them on its own, but that lacked style. Food chain: we outranked the rats, so we reserved the right to humiliate them.

Dad stopped home for a few minutes in between first and second whistle to check on Mom and get an apple for supper. He went into the bedroom to see her, and then he popped his head out the window. He hadn't shaved in a couple days, which made him seem older and weaker. "You boys want me to make you some eggs?"

"No, thanks," I said. "We'll eat later."

"Roman?" Dad said, but Roman didn't seem to hear him.

"Love you boys," he said and squeezed my shoulder.

"What if they don't eat it?" I asked later, even though we both knew it was a stupid question. Rats will eat anything. A rat will eat beef so rancid it's turned blue. A rat will chew through PVC pipe just to get at the raw sewage inside. Imagine the most disgusting thing possible, and rats will eat it.

Roman just kept glaring down at that door like a sniper waiting on his mark.

Finally, it burst open and the trash bag came flying out. It plopped on the asphalt next to the dumpster, but Old Irish didn't even bother to come out and move it.

"We're up," Roman said.

We sat at the kitchen table with the sausage slop, separating it into two trash bags. In one bag Roman poured a heap of potassium permanganate, which was these little purple crystals about the size of shucked sunflower seeds. In the other bag I poured the antifreeze, almost the whole gallon. "Now mix," he said, and we dug our hands into the bags. I mixed the one with the antifreeze, and it felt like a bag full of eyeballs and mud. "Keep to your side," Roman said.

Mom poked her head out the bedroom door. She looked exhausted but also like she had just woken up. "Boys, what's that smell?"

"Just a little science homework," Roman said. "Go back to bed."

"Just be careful now," Mom said and disappeared again.

Roman finished mixing up his bag and looked over at me. "Let's pick it up."

"When do you think mom is going to get better?" I asked. She just sort of vanished from us one day. That was the hardest part. Nothing specific seemed to trigger it. She just quit, which I think we both took to mean we did something wrong even if we wouldn't admit it to each other.

Roman walked over to the sink to scrub his hands. "Never. But there's nothing wrong with her in the first place."

I didn't agree with that, but Roman seemed so strong and mean right then that I didn't want to say so.

"Fucked in the head. No fixing that."

"Well, Dad thinks—"

"Dad's on his own now."

"Yeah, but—"

"Out of juice. Kaput. Car with a dead battery."

None of it seemed right to me. What could make a person just quit like that?

We went out onto the fire escape again. Roman tossed the first bag over the rail, the one with the potassium permanganate. I was getting ready to toss my bag over when he grabbed my arm. "Be patient."

The rats came. We couldn't see them, too dark, but we could hear them tearing through the plastic bag, ruffling like it was caught up in the wind. And they chirruped their angry little mating chirrups while they ate the sausage slop and potassium permanganate. They really will eat anything.

We looked down, unblinking, even though there was nothing to see. It was like standing in the middle of a field when it's black-out dark, no moon, and the wind is blowing. All that movement which seems to be coming from nowhere and everywhere all at once. You feel this awesome sort of power the world has, which also makes you feel small and weak.

When the sound died down and Roman was satisfied that they'd eaten up the first batch, he pointed to me, and I tossed the second bag over. I don't know what I expected, but time seemed to slow as we waited. The rats ate and chirruped, still as hungry and horny as ever. I could see small sliver of Roman's face in that light, and he just stared, didn't move or blink, just stared down at the alley. When the noise stopped again, nothing happened, and I was about to start asking him questions that were really more accusations, and that's when the little poofs of fire started, and before long they were all over the alley, gliding around like a hundred Japanese lanterns. They squealed these pathetic little squeals, more distinct and pathetic than their usual chirrups. Nothing quite so helpless as an animal in pain, even a rat.

Roman laughed like a madman. "Burn harder, you rat-fucks! Welcome to the Bronx!"

And they did burn. They scampered and wailed and burned, and we watched, mouths open at what we had done, what we were now capable of, each of us feeling some new power that had not existed in the world until that moment, not for us anyway.

"Would've worked better," Roman said, "if we added a third

part, diesel fuel or kerosene, something like that to sustain the burn." I hadn't realized until that moment how much time Roman had spent researching.

Mom opened the window. She looked down into the alley with us, confused like she usually was, more probably, but then she said, "My God. It's so pretty I could cry," which was the strange sort of thing she was always saying. She hugged her body as if she was cold even though it was normal Bronx September, which meant everything felt like armpit.

Then she started talking. "When I was a little girl," she said, "you know we lived over on Whittier Street, right next to that scrapyard. It was the dustiest, smelliest place I've ever been. They were supposed to stop working at ten p.m., but they never did. The owner installed these huge sodium lights, and they worked all night through. All the diesel fumes and rust smell. All that screeching metal and shouting. No quiet way to crush a car."

Roman and I both turned to Mom, who hadn't spoken so many words out loud in a year.

"*Those* were rats," she said, shaking her head at the memory. "We got them mixed up with cats a lot of times, that's how big they were. Sunday nights, the owner would shut things down and send his workers on out to hunt with shotguns. They stalked around the scrapyard with these spotlights which caught the reflection of eyes, and all night we'd hear shotgun blasts and squeal with terror while we hid under the bed. In the morning, there'd be a pile of the carcasses by the entrance, and people had to drive past it to sell their scrap. Then the owner would douse that rat pile with diesel and burn them up, and that smoke drowned the whole neighborhood. Everyone had to close their windows. Then they all went back to work, and then Sunday night came around again, and they went out into the yard to hunt. It never ended."

The alley had gone quiet, no more burning rats. They lay down there, charred up like potatoes tossed in a fire.

"When your father and I got married," Mom said, "we were so happy to get out of that neighborhood and into this one." With that, she turned and went back inside, and we didn't see her again for almost a week. It wasn't clear what she wanted us to take away from her story. That we were lucky? That she was sorry there were so many rats around? I think probably she was just talking, or trying to talk, the way people do sometimes.

"The fuck was that?" Roman said.

I shrugged.

When Mom left, this thick, suffocating silence draped itself over us. Nothing moved or squealed. No shuffling or scampering, no fire. I was suddenly desperate for the smallest squeak, the tiniest indication that perhaps two of the rats were still eating or still mating. It wasn't guilt exactly but a strange hollow feeling, and the vast hush that hung over the alley magnified everything. When you live in the middle of the city, quiet isn't a concept that ever occurs to you, it's white noise and shouts and honks all the time, and right then was the first time I'd ever noticed the quiet.

I didn't say much else to Roman after that. It was clear that he was satisfied, but something felt wrong to me, nagging like a stubbed toe. I collapsed onto our bed and closed my eyes and waited for the antenna in my brain to start picking up on the white noise of the city. It was there, but those screaming, burning rats toggled some switch, and I couldn't hear any of it. Just dead silence that tried to swallow me in one huge gulp. Pretty soon, I would relax, find my regular breathing pattern, start hearing all shouts and honks, the vast hum of the city, and only then would it feel like things had slipped back to normal. Then I started hearing the rats again, their sad little cries, their claws on the asphalt, the same noises we'd dealt with for years, like my brain was punishing me for what we'd done.

Roman came into bed soon, still breathing hard. I'm not sure if he'd been running some victory lap or if it was just the adrenaline of a mission accomplished. "Pretty badass," he said.

I pretended to be asleep, but he wasn't buying it.

He stripped down to his underwear and lay down next to me. "Must have been at least three dozen. Could have been more, won't know until tomorrow. But man, it worked, like *really* fucking worked."

"Right," I said. "It's science." All I could hear was the rats, louder than ever before. It's an unmistakable sound.

Roman's breaths seemed to get louder and louder, each one rocking the entire bed. I wasn't going to sleep anyway, but it bothered me.

"Roman," I said, "relax. Breathe."

"Can't," he said. "No way."

It was a strange sort of comedown he was dealing with right then, that lonely feeling that clings to you after you've accomplished something big and impressive. Now what? So the rats were gone? What would we do now, what would we hate now? What you don't realize is that hatred is like any other addiction, and when it's gone, you actually crave it. Without it, your world doesn't make much sense.

I hung in a dreamy state, not quite awake but not asleep either, until Dad came into our room after second whistle. "What did you boys do?" That's how I realized that the noises weren't in my head. They were back, little rat zombies. You don't get rid of rats, not ever. Maybe that's what Mom was trying to tell us.

We walked out to the fire escape.

"Jesus," Roman said, "what the hell?" meaning the sound of them all like a big rat army marching on the South Bronx.

We looked down into the darkness for a few minutes, hoping our eyes would adjust, but it was too dark. Dad shined a flashlight down then, a crummy one he rented from Old Irish, and we could see them all over the place, their flashing little eyes, more rats than ever, and what they were doing was eating their scorched little cousins, just devouring them. All that free protein, no way they'd waste it. No sentiment for a rat.

"Are they—?" Roman asked.

"Jesus," I said.

Dad peeked over the rail, down into the eerie half light of the alley. He didn't say anything or make any faces, just stared.

Roman turned the flashlight off and slumped down, just totally defeated. He'd used science. How could this happen?

And that was it. What I never told Roman, probably because I didn't quite realize it until years later, when I had my own kids and we lived over in Brooklyn Heights, is that I was glad the rats came back. For me, it was like stabilizing a wobbly orbit, like we needed their weight in our world to stay on track. They belonged somehow, and hating them belonged too. Hate something long enough, and that becomes the reason you hate it.

We stopped hunting the rats and finished out the school year. Roman got quieter, stopped stealing bikes and fighting so much. When August came, he decided he wouldn't go back to school, and pretty soon he took over Dad's job on first whistle, and Dad moved to second whistle. After that, life sped up, almost like we'd been searching for the on-ramp to the freeway, and then once we found it, we just set the cruise and went mile after mile without giving it any thought.

I went upstate for college. I studied engineering and worked in the dining hall and studiously avoided stories about home. In four years, I only came back once. When people asked, I just told them I was from the city. Roman never called, and even when I called him he never really said how things were going. Sometimes he'd mention the marines, but whenever I pushed him to go see a recruiter, he would just say, *Yeah, I'll have to do that soon*, but he never did. I wanted him to get away like I did, less for him and more for me. I was the prisoner who escapes by standing on his cellmate's shoulders.

There was a lake not far from campus, and it had a big stock of steelheads in it, so I took up fishing there. I knew a guy with a car and a fishing rod, and he let me borrow both, no rental fees. This was real nature, not a park surrounded by concrete, not the East River, which had the consistency of vegetable soup. Fishing is more like *not* doing something than it is like doing something. Your vision blurs and time slows and you hear the whir of nature all around, millions of unconnected sounds merging into something almost coherent. I'd sit there for hours, the heat of the sun on my shoulders until it just cooked me red, and I think I craved that sunburn, the way it would pulse and tingle as I lay in bed at night. It was the silence of waiting that I liked. Of course it was. I think we constantly try to recreate important moments, and we constantly fail at it. I was probably waiting there for the echo of that night with the rats, that final reverberation, just waiting for it to rebound through all the quiet, but it never did. It just hung there, like a suspended chord with no resolution in sight. I'd think about home, Roman and Dad passing each other on the way to work, but it wouldn't seem real, not in the middle of all that nature, and I eventually had to accept that I'd become just like Old Irish: it wasn't my rat problem either.

Then I started dating a girl from Clinton Hill, and we got serious enough to stop using condoms. That was a fresh feeling, nothing quite like it. She started asking questions about home and family. One night when we were drunk, I started telling her about Roman. I told her about the bikes he'd steal and the fights he'd pick and about Old Irish, and then I told her about the rats, the whole story, which I'd never told anyone else, and all she said was, *Well, just thank God you're here now*, as if I'd escaped from some concentration camp. I should have set her straight, but I didn't. We got married a few years later and moved near her family in Brooklyn.

Mom drowned in the bathtub during my last semester, or that was what Dad told everyone. I came home for the funeral, my first time since leaving, and I stepped off the train, and I could just feel the Bronx all around me, the noises and smells. We go off and change, but home always waits for us. Stay away long enough, though, and it starts to feel like returning to the scene of a crime.

I walked the length of the platform slowly, taking it all in. Dad was at the other end, just on the other side of the gate. He was squatting against the column, unshaven, wearing his dirty white jumpsuit, and I thought, *That's awfully nice of him to come meet me at the station right now*. His hair was grayer than I remembered, and he'd lost weight, and as I drew closer, I realized it was actually Roman. He had that hundred-mile stare to him, no telling how old he even was anymore, could have gone twenty years in either direction. The world seemed to have burned a hole straight through him while I was away. I stopped walking. For the first time in years, everything seemed to slow down again. I thought about that lake and the trout breaking the surface of the water, the silence, and I wanted to escape to there, all that quiet, because in ten seconds I was going to hug my brother and pull away, and then we'd be looking at each other, and I'd have to say something, but I had no idea what that would be.

Hide-and-Seek

What I do on Friday afternoons especially around the holidays is I take the bus out to the airport and have some drinks. I can sit at the bar with a Wild Turkey and pretend I'm flying to Fort Lauderdale for a weekend of nooky on a beach with a professional cheerleader named Traci. When people ask, that's just what I tell them. Traci can do the splits, you know, and she can do them *anywhere*! Two or three drinks, and I'm on that beach, and Traci is reading *Mademoiselle* in the lounger next to me. We're drinking rum out of coconuts and trying decide which is bluer, the sky or the water, and right then we have a good laugh because I just fondled her yum-yums and made that old-fashioned horn noise.

That guy has the life, people think. *Got his shit together, all right. Probably some kind of banker or politician. Traci is one lucky broad.*

And that's what I do. Always did have a good imagination.

Then, just the other day, I'm sitting in a bar right near the security lines, and I'm pretty well into my routine. That's when my brother Warren sits down at the other end of the bar. My real-life brother! He's wearing a suit jacket and carrying one of those little bags that's made just for computers. It's been ten years at least since we've talked, probably more than that. Who keeps track of these things?

Our eyes meet two or three times before he connects that

it's me, it's his brother sitting at the other end. "Jesus," he says. "Johnny?" and I say, "Yep. It's me, and it's you too." He grabs his little computer purse and his drink, and he moves next to me. He eyes me for a minute, like this is just too impossible. He takes a drink. Then he reaches his hand out, and I shake it.

"So what the hell anyway?"

"Business," I say and twist my glass around, which breaks apart the cocktail napkin. "Slammed these days. Real busy."

"That's good, that's good. Busy is good."

"Cheers to that," I say and we raise our glasses but only a couple inches. "Business for you too?"

"No," he says. "Not for once. Off to Aruba for the week."

"Wow," I say and then sit there trying to remember if Aruba is Mediterranean or Caribbean and if Caribbean is the one by Italy or the one with Jamaica.

He waves down the bartender. "Put them both on mine," he says. Then he turns back to me and says, "Yeah, so Aruba. Meeting a friend there. She went a couple days ago, but I couldn't get away. Clients everywhere you look. You know how it gets."

"Clients," I say and shake my head the way people do. I'm suddenly aware of my fat, callused hands, all cracked open from working a tow truck in winter. I'm not sure who *she* is. He either got married or divorced about seven years ago; I heard that from someone. So it could be his old lady, or he could have himself a Traci.

Truth is, my brother and me, we always hated each other. To begin with, you need to know that Peter, our other brother, he died when we were still kids. Nobody ever really got over that. Peter and I shared a room, but since we didn't have space in the apartment to stow his bed, and since Mom and Dad wouldn't sell it to some idiot stranger, they left it in our bedroom, like the carcass of some big dumb animal. Then Mom and Dad got divorced, and I thought that would be the end of my dead brother's bed, but Dad took it to his new place down in Dorchester and made me sleep in it every other weekend. Warren got a brand new futon.

"You deserve it," Warren kept saying. "You killed Peter," which is absolutely not what happened. It was a car accident.

I'm sitting there thinking about Peter and about his bed and Warren's futon. I'm ignoring whatever Warren is saying about Aruba. "You killed Peter, you little shitbird," he told me. "You wanted your own room, so you killed him." He kept saying that; years he said it. Hear that enough, and you start to believe it. All the mean older brother stuff he did like handcuffing me to bike racks or taking a big wet dump in my church loafers, but saying that was the worst.

"So are you living in the same place now?" he asks, meaning that basement craphole over in Eastie, the one that smelled so bad when it rained, like hydraulic cement and wet collie. He came over for a minute after Mom's or Dad's funeral, I don't remember which.

I drink the rest of my drink and push it toward the edge. I figure if he's buying. I tell him no, that I'm moving to Beacon Hill soon, thinking of buying a place there as soon as I can find one with twelve-foot ceilings.

"Sounds like things are really coming together." He shoots his cuffs then so that he can check his watch, and his cuff links are these old brass things, tarnished. It looks like something was painted on them, maybe a frosted cupcake or a hyena, but it's worn off. If he wants to make a big show of things like that, shooting his cuffs like Whitey Bulger, he needs to spring for some new ones.

Warren's cell phone rings, and I can tell he wants to answer, but it seems impolite, me being right there. "Go ahead," I say, and he does. He walks over to the big windows overlooking the tarmac and covers his other ear. I watch him for a minute, and then I order us a couple of shots. "Crown Special Reserve," I tell the bartender. "My brother's favorite. Make them doubles." She brings them, and I shoot mine right away, and I'm reaching for the other one when the bartender turns my way and sees me and gets this suspicious look on her face, like maybe I'm some sort of lying kidnapper with mean sex fetishes. She keeps looking over in my direction, won't turn away, and then Warren comes back and says, "What's this?" and I say, "She brought us a couple on the house." I wink and make a moaning sort of sex face so he gets the idea.

Peter died at Christmas. I begged Dad to get a real tree like they had in *It's a Wonderful Life*. For once, he listened to me. We took the station wagon to this place way down on the South Shore. We had to rent a saw for a dollar extra, which pissed Mom off since we had one back at home. We stomped through these long lines of trees, playing hide-and-seek. Peter and me kept being the hiders, and for once we were winning. It was so dark and there were so many trees that you could hide and then circle back to a new spot. Warren got real mad about how hard we were to find, so every time he found one of us, he tackled us. Then Peter and me tackled him back one time, and Warren gut-punched me, and I cried, and Dad yelled at us, and that was the end of hide-and-seek. That's who Warren always was, the kind of brother who knew how to throw a punch but not how to take one. But man, if I didn't think about punching him back that whole ride home, catching him unawares while he sat next to me. Sometimes I still pretend we never tackled Warren that night, which means it would have taken us couple minutes longer at the Christmas tree place, and what happened next never actually happened at all.

On the way back home the tree shifted loose from the roof and fell into the other lane and another car swerved right into us, which killed Peter and nobody else. He got rushed to the hospital and they did surgery on him, but it didn't work. Mom crumpled to the floor and bawled like somebody was torturing her until the nurse came out and walked her to a separate room. Dad just got real quiet and stared at the wall for an hour, even when the doctor came out and asked him to sign some forms that made Peter officially dead. It seemed like he didn't even breathe or blink.

The tree got tossed on the side of the road, but the day after Peter's funeral, Dad went back to the site with our saw and carved it up into foot-long chunks. He made me go with him to help, but he wouldn't say a word, wouldn't even look at me. For the next couple years, he sat on his front porch and whittled those chunks down into nothing, just shavings that stuck to the soles of our shoes. We'd track them back home to Mom's, where she yelled at us for being such messy boys, but when we told her what the shavings were, she cried and said, "Your father."

Warren and me drink in silence and watch people. There's this family of five trying to go through security, but the kids are running around, playing space ninja or something, and saying *Kapow!* at each other, and the mom looks like she's about ready to start throwing punches at whoever gets close enough. I'm feeling pretty drunk. It seems like everything is whirring around, people and sounds and even the smells from the coffee stand next to us, all of it blending together. I can feel everything all at once. After a while, Warren says, "It really has been too long. We shouldn't be like that."

"Like what?"

"Like strangers."

I nod, but I don't say anything else. I'm feeling numb and good. The light in the terminal is just right and it smells fresh. I start thinking about how I should really get back at Warren. Gut-punch him maybe. "Now we're even, shitbird!" I'd say.

"I should probably brave security here pretty soon," Warren says.

"Right," I say. "Me too. I always put it off till the last minute."

"We could brave it together."

"Well," I say. The bartender comes over. "One more?" I say, thinking that'll help me get my courage up. Even now Warren's my big brother.

We drink and avoid eye contact for a while. We're strangers at a bar. It's supposed to be easier to talk to strangers in a bar. There are these people all around us, this blurred commotion, and it makes me feel like we have this privacy, like we're in a tent. Warren's movements get slower. When he picks up his whiskey, the napkin sticks to the underside, but he doesn't seem to notice. I get really mad at him for that. *Just peel the fucking napkin off!* I want to shout. Who wants to go to Aruba with a guy who acts like that? Then he starts talking in a low voice, not quite a whisper, but hushed, private. "I wish we did this more."

"Me too," I say.

"Do you? You don't hate me?"

"You're my brother."

"That's right," he says. "I am. That's something, isn't it?"

"That's a lot."

Warren is drunker than I am. His eyes get wide and sad, like a big dumb cow. As much I want to punch him then, there's a right time and a wrong time to punch your older brother, I do know that. You can't punch sad people, that's a rule. He leans toward me more. "I always thought you hated me. You always loved Peter more."

"Peter and I shared a room," I say.

He swipes at the air between us. "Don't be a shit. Why can't you just admit it?"

"It always seemed like us against you," I say. "I don't know why."

"Peter would be fifty this year," he says like he didn't hear me, "did you know that?"

I didn't, but I lie, Yes, I did, of course I did. Peter and me were awfully close. "It's been a long time."

"Fifty fucking years old. Dead for forty-one." He shakes his head and rattles the ice in his empty glass until the bartender looks over. For a minute I think he might cry. A thousand people around us, coming and going, living their lives next to each other but not really with each other, and my older brother who I always hated, he was right about that, drinking whiskey and crying. It's sad, but my brother and me can only really talk about three or four different things, and one of them is our dead brother. It's sad how I can't punch him either, or maybe how I don't really want to anymore. I guess I've always wanted to know someone else was still miserable about all of it, but now that it's happening, it's a nasty business. Big brothers aren't supposed to cry, but little brothers aren't supposed to be dead either, I guess.

Warren leans forward into his hands, and I can see the grease stains under his fingernails. I don't even know what business he's in now, but I do know what grease under the fingernails means. "Can I tell you a secret?" he says. "I wasn't as sad at mom's funeral or at dad's as I was a Peter's. Isn't that awful?" He rubs his face the way you do when you need to shave or when you're too drunk. His cuff links pop out again, and that's when I recognize them. They were Dad's. Dad always wore them to church, which was the only time he ever had to dress up nice.

"No," I tell him. "I don't think it's so bad. Peter was a real sweet kid."

"Remember how you wouldn't sleep anywhere else but Peter's bed? How Dad even took it to the new apartment when he moved out?"

"What do you mean?" I ask, but even as I'm saying it, I do remember. Dad kept the bed for me. There was another person in the room a lot of those nights, too, I remember that. I'm not saying I believe in ghosts or something dumb like that, but I wasn't alone. I'd call out and look all over the place, but I'd never find him. I needed him to help me against Warren, but he was gone. I guess I gave up on him at some point, and I guess Warren wants me to feel guilty about that. Some people never do change.

"I need to hit the head," I say, and I get up. "I'll be right back, and we'll go through security together." Warren's too drunk to notice I don't have a bag. He staring down at his drink, and I step behind him and raise up my fists, and I'm about ready to get even, one big haymaker right into the curve of his neck, but the bartender looks my way again, that goddamned bartender, and I have to run off and hide.

I go over at the far side of the security lines and stand in the middle of all the strangers and watch my brother. He's looking down into his glass like it's a telescope. It's five minutes, and he doesn't move. I can't tell if he's sleeping or trying to keep from crying or if he's just thinking real hard. He finally jerks awake when they call his flight, what I think has to be his flight: 2142 to Miami, Florida. Can't even afford direct. He grabs his bag and takes off toward security. He starts looking around, every direction, but he can't tell me from all the strangers in line. He stumbles over to the bathroom and then comes out looking real confused. For a minute, I fantasize about stomping out there and tackling him but I don't. I stay hidden in the crowd, and he eventually moves off, trying to make his flight. The whole time he's in line, he keeps looking around, but I don't ever show myself. He's probably going on vacation alone, which is just sad. I'm sad for him even though he's always been so horrible to me.

He'll be fine. We'll forget about each other for a few years, forget we still have a brother left. And things do have a way of getting better. They did after Peter died; it just took a while. They will now. Pretty soon I'll be in a new apartment, one with wall-to-wall and a dishwasher. It'll have laundry, or at least I'll be close enough to walk to the Laundromat. Lately I've been thinking about running for something. School board, maybe. I'd like to help out all those kids. And someday soon I'll be sitting in a lawn chair in front of my door, like Dad used to, only I'll be reading the latest polling numbers, and right then some young tart with pouty lips will walk right over to me and say, *Hello, there, kitten, I'm Traci.*

Country Lepers

My wife moved in with you last month. You, a bald museum docent. Surely you know the story by now.

She comes home from the library at six or so, and I'm still running sausage through the grinder and sheathing them into the casings and twisting them at eight-inch intervals until I get the long sausage trains like in the cartoons. I have the air conditioner cranked up, even though it's almost November. Gus, our Irish Setter, I have tied up on the sidewalk, and he's staring at me through the window. I'm just churning out the sausages, hanging lengths from cupboard doors and the refrigerator handle and the backs of chairs. It's a one-bedroom apartment, so there's sausage everywhere, even in our bedroom, even hanging from the curtain rod in the bathroom. Everything smells like fresh sausage. I have to do this from home since I let my lease on the shop over in Turtle Bay lapse last month.

Well, this part you've probably heard about already, but here's how it actually happened. Karen walks in with Gus, and they both see these sausages hanging on everything. She can't even turn on the living room lamp without brushing up against a knackwurst. And Gus starts bucking around, trying to get at anything he can, and his hair is wafting about the whole apartment.

"Marty," Karen says, "get your sausages out of our bedroom right now!"

And I tell her it can't be helped but that I will soon. It's a couple grand worth of sausage hanging around here, and I'll have it in cold storage by morning. But right now she needs to get the dog out or he'll have a seizure from too much excitement.

"I'm not sleeping here with this smell tonight," she says. "Get the sausage out!"

"Karen," I say while I crank on the grinder, "This is my job. I have to. You know that." Gus is still flailing around, and Karen has to hold his leash up high, above her head, to keep him from getting at all that meat.

She stares at me for a long time. Just stares, this mean, ugly stare that says *Marty, I want to pound your face into ground mutton*. I've never seen this from her before and didn't know she was capable of it. She's a librarian, but you know that.

I just keep on grinding out the sausage links, casing them up, twisting, and hanging. I have thirty pounds left, and I'm not wasting it. It's my job. You have a job, so you understand, I'm sure. I wouldn't tell you to stop docenting little kids at the museum. I wouldn't tell her to stop shelving her books.

So she leaves. She puts Gus in my station wagon, and she leaves. In the morning, I find a note taped to the mailbox, detailing the atrocities I've inflicted upon her for the past six years: how I always smelled like I'd just rolled around in a bucket of intestines; how we were probably the only people in New York who consistently had pepperoni logs stacked on the nightstand; how I was in our bathroom one time, brushing my teeth while her cousin was showering, and I tripped and fell into the curtain and ripped it off the hook and then had to break my fall, and one of my hands ended up grazing her nipple on the way down. There are others, but you get the idea. She hasn't been happy for years, our Karen. Apparently I'm like a contagion, and she should have quarantined herself a long time ago. She feels infected by me. And did I realize we haven't even made love for over a year? It's as if we just forgot to have kids. Mostly, we're just a bad fit, always have been. Square peg, rhombus hole. Close, but a little cockeyed. She's cosmopolitan, I'm rural.

But you, the bald museum docent—you're quiet and kind, and you make her sizzle with life again. You keep your beard trimmed and watch Charlie Rose. You own a shoe polish kit and never eat fried catfish. She can't waste any more time being unhappy and childless with me. Sizzle, she says. *Do please understand.*

And I know what you're probably wondering: Did her cousin have big nipples? Well, I'm not talking on that.

The apartment is in her name. She makes most of the payments, and I can't stay. I'd like to help you out, Marty, she says when I call to talk it over, but we're moving to his place in Gramercy, and we need the equity to expand. Do please understand.

She never used to talk like that—*Do please understand*—but apparently you bald museum docents talk like snooty assholes, and you've already started to rub off on her.

Since you've evicted me from my apartment, I scan the *Post* for a new place, spend an hour calling around. Lots of places have been rented already, which makes me think I should learn how to use the Internet at some point. A studio in Hell's Kitchen is listed at $1,600 a month, and this is close enough to Gramercy for me to occasionally bump into you in a planned-accidental sort of way.

"Any chance we could negotiate on the price?" I say to the woman. "I'm pretty handy. Can fix leaky pipes and trim you a nice pork shoulder each week."

"How much were you thinking?"

"I could swing $800 a month," I say. But even that would be pretty tight. Gus would have to eat squirrels from the park.

Then I try a studio over in Hoboken, but it's still over $1,000 a month. The first thing I think is, No way I'm paying that much to live in New Jersey. I'd imagine living in Hoboken is a lot like standing on a balcony that overlooks a killer party. And telling people you live there is a lot like telling them you have Ebola. But you know all about the Jersey issue. You live in Gramercy.

Then I find an ad from out in Changewater. Way out in western Jersey, not far from where I grew up. I don't want to move that far away, but I also didn't want my wife to drop me and start playing kiss-me-where-I-pee with one of you bald museum docents. This is what the ad reads: *Quiet NJ Livestock Farm. No noise, no polutn. One month labor for one room to sleep. No kids, no yap-dogs.* I call. I can tell it's an old man because he speaks slowly and sounds angry that he's still alive. And he clicks his teeth, adjusting his dentures. It's an unmistakable sound, like ice clinking into a glass. My father used to do it. "It's a nice enough piece of land," he says. "You have to work it with me. That's the deal."

Apparently his daughter takes care of him, but she's a teacher and is leading a group of snot-noses on a trip to Europe for an entire month. He'll trade a month's rent for a month's work.

"Changewater," I say. "Is that near Califon?"

"No," he says. "Near Hampton."

"Oh," I say. "Near Asbury."

"No," he says. "It's near Hampton."

And that's how he talks. Kind of refreshing compared to you bald museum docent types but still kind of enough to make you want to murder his fucking rooster.

Then he tells me I can't be a city priss, have to be willing to kill hogs and fix fence rails and do other man-type work that you couldn't even spell. And I tell him that's why I called, that I grew up nearby, and I run a butcher shop in the city. I can swing an axe and pull nails and hang drywall if he needs it. I can probably even show him a few things about butchering. I'm the perfect tenant for his situation. It's lucky our paths crossed.

"I don't like city people," he says. "You live there long enough you forget how to do anything but eat cheese and talk about paintings."

"I do have a dog," I say. "The ad says no pets."

"No," he says. "It says no yappy dogs. Is it a real dog or the kind that rides around in a purse?"

His name is Linus Houghton. Have you ever met a Linus? Or are they all Reginalds and Chesterfields at the museum? He walks with a jerky limp and has a splotchy, squished sort of face that looks a lot like a tomato left in the sun for a week. He's short and wiry and has perfect posture. He rarely speaks, but he sometimes gets this mischievous grin on his face, like he farted on your pillow when you weren't looking.

His place is tucked way off the main road, halfway up a hill and with thickets all around. Can't even see there's a house from the road. Driving up the long lane is like driving through the Holland Tunnel. The trees overhang and actually catch on the roof of my station wagon. Then I emerge into a wide swathe of pasture, hilly and green and muddy, bordered by a rickety split-rail fence. Hogs I can't see but I can smell. Sheep in the far pen and a few cattle beyond them. And for a moment it's refreshing, like walking back into my childhood. That smell.

This is the thing, bald museum docent: I slowly became one of those New Yorkers who never left the island. I made jokes about Jersey and sometimes wore a scarf. I stopped eating so much bologna. Thought playing the part might infect my blood somehow, squeeze the rustic out of me, morph me into a better husband somehow. I would have done way worse for our Karen. No such luck. She found you at some point. God knows when, but clearly long before the sausage incident. Probably closer to the nipple incident.

But here I am now, back in the country, breathing air so clear it feels cold as it hits my lungs. It reminds me real air shouldn't smell like soy sauce and burnt Styrofoam.

Linus stands on the porch. An unlit, hand-rolled cigarette hangs from his lips, and he talks as if he doesn't even notice it there.

"You New York?"

I nod and reach out my hand to him. "Marty," I say. He turns around and leads me inside. It's an original farmhouse: creaky floorboards, cracking wallpaper, that earthy smell that makes me wonder if he keeps a closet full of dirt somewhere.

"Your daughter is gone for a month?" I say.

He points to a bedroom. "Right here," he says. "Get changed into something you don't mind smelling like hog guts." He limps away.

There's a four-poster twin bed in the middle of the room with crocheted pillowcases and a stack of quilts on the chair in the corner. It reminds me of my old bedroom. We didn't have so much land as Linus seems to, but it was fine. I haven't been back there in ten years, not since my father caught the extra-bad variety of ass cancer and we had to sell it to pay for his treatments. That's when I moved to the city, met our Karen, and opened a butcher shop. Somewhere in between all of that, I had to move the shop to our apartment, and I also accidentally touched my cousin-in-law's nipple. But those sorts of details start to blend together now that Karen is knocking boots with you.

I turn Gus loose in the yard, and he bolts off after some critter in the brush, just like he does in the park. He'll come back after a bit, though. He gets nervous when he hasn't sniffed me for a while.

Linus has a slaughter pen set up, right next to the hogs. Seems cruel to kill a boar right in front of his cousins, but it's convenient, and a hog doesn't know murder from a rusty carburetor choke. They'll even drink each other's blood if you don't separate them.

We stack the wood under the tub and light it and let it start bringing the water to a boil. Then Linus ties the hog off and pops him in the head with a .22 long and we roll him over and jab a knife into the sternum and twist to snag that main artery. We cinch him to the block and tackle, hoist him up over the blood pan, head down. I stop to watch him bleed out for a minute until I feel Linus glaring at me. I haven't done the actual slaughtering for a long time, and I forgot how much blood there is. The way its mouth hangs open makes it look like it's trying to squeal or gasp for air. We don't speak, just work like we ran out of things to say twenty years ago.

Soon we're scalding him and dragging the bell scrapers over him to rip the hair and scurf off all the way. That's the dirty work. Nothing like that stringy hog fur stuck to everything, kind of like pubic hair rolled in diarrhea and bacon grease. Probably why I stopped slaughtering them and just did the fine butchering. Once, when I was about seventeen, my father and I slaughtered a sow during the day, and then I took a girl out to the drive-in that night—her name was Brenda—and we were kissing with lots of tongue, and I was working on her bra when she noticed the dark scurf residue stuck under my nails and knuckle creases. I'd showered and used Lava soap and everything, but it's hard to get rid of that stuff, and naturally, Brenda, who lived in town, screamed every combination of fear and hatred, and I never did get to see her jugs, which was bad enough, but I also had the kind of woody that was so puckered and veiny it actually hurt. You know the kind. You probably get those for our Karen, don't you? Even now, feeling the scurf on my skin gives me this strange sensation of anger and shame and arousal that I fear Linus will somehow notice.

It's near dark before we've pulled the kidneys and heart and other organs out. Linus doesn't want to hang him overnight even though I tell him the pork will have a richer flavor.

"It ages just the same," he says. He clicks his dentures. "Lazy city people."

I don't want him thinking I'm lazy, so I start to hack him up and wrap the shanks and hocks and ribs and loins. My father was the best butcher I ever knew, cleaned every scrap, could squeeze an extra cut from a steer's nose and make it taste like sirloin. Linus isn't so talented, but he does okay. I show him a few things, about dipping the blade in cold water and keeping it moving with long strokes, about pitching it at the proper angles, about staying with the grain as long as possible. He pretends not to listen to me. "Don't play smart," he says. But before long he's moving faster and not wasting so much. Mostly I can tell he's the kind of man who does everything himself. I imagine if I kept after him long enough, he could teach me how to make rocks. And he doesn't seem to tire. He hangs that hand-rolled cigarette from his dry lips and sets to work, never lighting it, just clenching it there and slowly chewing out the tobacco. And he's quiet in a sturdy old man sort of way, so quiet it makes you feel like a sissy when you start talking, like he outlasted you in some primal game of chess.

"I could take some of this into the city," I tell him. "Sell it for higher than market price. SoHo. Gramercy. Midtown West—those people love overpaying for anything."

Linus stares at me for a minute. He doesn't talk, just clenches that cigarette between his lips. "You trying to steal my pork?"

"No, sir," I say, and I go back to work.

We slaughter two hogs a day for the first three days. "You do okay with that," Linus says, "so we'll stick with it. Don't want to confuse you."

Evenings, when we're finished working, I drive back into the city. It's a strange sensation: I don't miss the place, but I'm just so used to being there, it's like there's a gravitational pull I can't escape. Kind of like having a limp that slowly heals. You know, how you end up hobbling longer than you have to because you just get used to it? Gus isn't thrilled about the situation. He obeys when I open the car door and toss his leash in there, but in that lackadaisical, snooty way that reminds me he's a teenager in dog years. At first, we head toward the natural history museum. I want to sniff you out, see the guy who's putting it to my wife.

I pretend Gus is a seeing-eye dog and that I'm blind, and I get away with it longer than you'd think. Just stick an arm in front and pretend to be groping for something. No one wants to question a blind man. But I'm sure they realize I can see just fine when I stare at this exhibit of early Neanderthals hunting a woolly mammoth. It says not to touch, and I don't, but boy, do I want to peel back the little huntress's tunic, get a peek at her chest. But I realize I'm an idiot. That kind of thing has gotten me into trouble before—touching someone else's nipple, which I swear was mostly an accident—and I guess touching the Neanderthal tit wouldn't really be sticking it to you the way I'd like. And that's really all I was after. On my way out, I ask the blue-blazered docent if one of his colleagues is bald and talks like a pretentious member of

Parliament, but he ignores me. You can understand why, I guess. I wonder now, did they tell you about me later as you sat in your break room, eating your camembert and rye crackers?

I'm running low on money, so I grab some cheap Chinese noodles for dinner. Gus and I end up in Gramercy, wandering the streets. I mutter to myself, thinking of the things I can say when I do bump into the both of you. "Karen," I could say and remove my hat. "Look at all this hair!" Or I could tell her I'll start refilling the ice trays and taking her for bacon and pancakes on Saturdays. Or I could say something about not being a fossil, like you are, but I can't quite work out the phrasing, and I'm afraid I'll get it wrong and seem like an idiot rural who also happens to have a full head of hair.

I wander the side streets and alleys until I see her car—our car. The little Honda hatchback you're probably embarrassed about. It's on a tight one-way right next to the private park, surrounded by Volvos and Audis and glossy black iron fences. I can't decide if I want to sit on it and wait for her or slash the tires. Gus sniffs around the doors because he smells her and probably thinks that means he'll get some food. So I wait for almost an hour, leaning against the car, planning my move. I have to be back to the farm in the morning, and it's a long drive. So I tear off a corner of the Chinese leftover box and leave a note under the windshield wiper: *Let's talk*, I write. *Gus and I miss you. Call me.* Then I write down the number from Linus Houghton's ad and start on my drive.

It's not like Karen and I ever had such a good thing going. Bad match from the start. You probably don't realize, though. Probably don't ask too many questions about me. You're a bald museum docent, used to doing the talking. She wanted to train me into some refined fop who liked art and Russian opera, you see, and I was pretty reluctant. She's so quiet and refined. Reads all those books and never talks too loud in a restaurant, even when I wear a flannel shirt under that Joseph Abboud sport coat she bought me. I do think she loved me at first. She was a city kid, grew up in a boxy Bronx high-rise, and here I was, a guy with calluses. She could feel cultured around a guy like that. Looking back, she probably started getting frustrated early on, though, when she realized I wasn't going to turn into some cosmopolitan dick.

Has she told you any of this? Told you about our silent fights, sitting across from each other at that little metal table we had, eating cold pastrami sandwiches, just glaring? Or what about all those nights we just threw our hands up and went to sleep because we were too tired to fight anymore? Or that President's Day weekend, 1993, when we drove up to Vermont, to that adorable little bed and breakfast with the wraparound porch and the gingerbread trim. It had a petting zoo—cows, sheep, a couple pigs, a horse. All she wanted to do was feed the lambs, run her fingers through their soft coat, and so why did I go on explaining about how the different parts she was petting were really just different cuts? *That's the scrag right there, dear. Kind of tough but okay for stew. And that— that's the fillet. I like the chump chops better, a little fattier, but most people like the fillet. That's what you'd order at the little restaurant down the street—the one you said took reservations six months out and we would never get to try.* She was awfully upset after that, which is probably fair. I apologized and everything, told her I'd take her to get that fillet soon, though I never did. Later that night she crawled on top of me and started gyrating. And I just went with it because who wouldn't? Even you would. But halfway through I realized she wasn't moaning so much as she was sobbing, and then I didn't know what to do, so I sat there for a minute before I started feeling dirty. Then I rolled her over and we sat quietly in the dark and didn't talk for a while.

On the drive home she told me I was like a chunk of deformed brass. She kept polishing me, thinking I'd stay like that. I'd be like gold. But after a couple weeks I'd be all tarnished again, and she'd have to start over. That's called a metaphor, and she uses lots of those, being a librarian and all.

I wonder, did she tell you some skewed version of this? Or was she maybe too embarrassed? Or does my name not even come up?

I start suspecting something is wrong with Linus late that first week. We're up early mending fence, splitting firewood, clearing brush from trails in the woods. It's all refreshing work, and I'm taken back immediately to being a kid, trolling around the farm with my father, working those thick yellow calluses deep into the creases of my hands. And Linus starts to open up just a little, easing off the angry old man routine.

"A museum docent?" he says.

"A bald one," I tell him.

He shakes his head. "Never been to a museum myself."

"Well," I say. But I don't really tell him much more about you since I don't know much more. Just that you guide little kids around and don't have as much hair as I do.

"So when you drive in there at night, it's what, some kind of stalking?"

"Nothing like that," I tell him, but then I don't really explain any more since I don't know why exactly I do go in there or what I'd do if I bumped into you.

Anyway, while we're mending a length of split-rail and talking like this, Linus reaches too far for a flat-blade screwdriver, and his forearm pops out from under his jacket. And it's messy looking: red and blistered, dark splotches like craters. Mix that with his old man wrinkles, and it starts to look like someone hit him with a load of buckshot and he never cleaned it, so it got all gangrened. Has to hurt like a real bastard.

Linus catches me staring, I know he does, and we both stop for just a minute. He looks down at his exposed arm, but he doesn't cover it because that would be too obvious.

"What you do," he says, "is buy her some sort of jewelry. A necklace, maybe, with a turquoise rock on it. Women love turquoise shit."

"Right," I say.

He stands and stretches, kind of nonchalant like, pulls his shirt back over his forearm. "You've been working out good," he says.

"You go hard, don't need me training you. How's an extra hundred a week sound? On top of room and board."

I squint at him, trying to figure his angle, but I don't think too long. I need the money, and I tell him that'd be great if he can spare it.

"It's a deal," he says. "A hundred a week for the next few weeks so long as you keep working out. Get you back on your feet, maybe help you buy a turquoise rock."

I leave Gus with Linus that night when I drive in to the city. They seem to have hit it off: Gus gets his snout scratched, but he doesn't ask stupid human questions, doesn't stare at that rotting arm. As I drive that night, I can all but see Gus with his face on Linus's lap, the old man's gruesome looking arm draped around him, petting little circles, feeding him chunks of bologna while they listen to the radio.

I park near Baruch College and walk up and down the side streets until I see the little hatchback that you hate. At first I'm dismayed because it looks like my note is still stuck under the wipers, but then I realize it's a different note, one from Karen. *Please, Marty*, it says. *Don't come around. Vick carries a stun rod for work, and I don't want him to use it on you. Hugs to Gus, Karen.*

What's odd, though, is how small *to Gus* is, like she wrote *Hugs* as a sign-off but then realized it was inappropriate now and had to squeeze the other part in to make it more acceptable. I stare at it for a long time, how squished *to Gus* is.

So I write her another note on the back of hers, and I pin it under the wiper blade: *Dogs can't hug, but I can. Call me. This is silly.*

We trade more notes on the car. Karen doesn't call, but she responds. One of them says it's not fair to her, the way I'm writing nice notes now, that I have to stop. It's like I'm Lopakhin and she's Lyuba, and we're trying to keep on living in some cherry orchard even though we know we can't. She knows I don't read books like she does, but she still says things like that. Please do stop, Martin, she says.

You're oblivious to all of this, of course. No way she's telling you. *Do please understand, Vick, I'm just writing little notes to Marty, but you're still the one who gets to see my nipples.*

I ask Linus if his daughter has any books around so I can find out about Lopakhin.

"What?" he says.

"Doesn't she have some books around here or something?"

He looks confused. "Oh," he says. "My daughter. No. No books."

Then he limps outside and calls for Gus. And I sit there wondering about Linus, what his deal really is. He's a mysterious character, and I think I could live in his house for the next ten years and still not really understand him. Why he is how he is. That arm, his daughter, all of it. I think on that for a while, and I can't decide who I'm more like, Linus or you. I guess neither. I'm some strange mixture who only erects half walls around himself. And I don't know where that leaves me, where I should be or who I should be there with.

So I go to the library one evening, tired of talking around the issue. I'll make Karen tell me about Lopakhin, why I'm like him. But she's not there. Must have changed her schedule to eat dinner with you.

I ask a different librarian about Lopakhin. She helps me find this book, *The Cherry Orchard*, and I read half that damn thing to find out about him. He seems like a superior-type dick who really isn't. The kind of guy who drinks tea and would never cheer for the Mets because it wouldn't be proper, even though he wants to. But I guess that's the point. She likes the refined assholes who get offended by paper napkins and buy new furniture designed to look old. So when I write her a note back, I mention something about how Lopakhin cares about Lyuba, you can tell he does, and isn't that worth something?

Then Linus's daughter apparently has a problem with her passport, and so she has to stay in Madrid a bit longer. He wants to know, could I maybe do the same? Maybe an extra week? He could use the help before winter sets in. And he'd be willing to up it to two hundred dollars that extra week.

I tell him sure, I could use the time to set up another place. I don't say anything about his daughter even though I want to. My role with Linus is pretty limited. I need the money, and he's offering enough that I keep my mouth shut. I tell him I can stay even longer if he needs it. I look down at his arm, the nasty one with the boils. I don't mean to, but I can't help it because I'm sure me being here helps a load, what with that arm being so torn up.

"No," he says. "Just a week."

It's getting colder now, thick frost in the mornings, but we still head out just after sunrise. Most mornings we spend out a ways from the house, splitting firewood. At first he insists on working the chainsaw himself while I drop the logs in the hydraulic splitter and stack them in the truck bed. But I can tell he's struggling with it. And so I offer to switch spots.

"I can handle a chainsaw just fine," I say. "Used to all the time. Why not let me take over, give your bad arm a rest."

He glares at me then, like I just insulted him. "My what?" he says.

"It's why I'm here, right?" I say.

"Your wife doesn't like you too much," he says. "That's why." Then he drops the chainsaw at his feet and motions for me to take over.

We go on like this for most of the morning, cutting up the better part of three maples without saying a word. Near noon, when the sun has peaked out just a bit, Linus rolls up his sleeves in a big, dramatic scene, as if to signal he can do whatever he likes now. And both arms are splotched with lesions and open sores and this white sort of mold-looking stuff all around them.

"Stare now," Linus says. "Get it out of your system."

And then I don't know what to do. Do I stare or not? And so I just glance over real quick, as if I see but don't really care too much one way or the other. I feel Linus staring at my back, but I just keep on cutting away, the sawdust blowing out the back end, clinging to my arm hair and every little crook in my body.

That night we're eating pork chops and applesauce when Linus tells me he won't be needing me that extra week after all. His daughter sorted out the passport problem. She'll be back in a few days. I should pack my things.

I stare at him for a while. He doesn't look at me, just keeps chomping away at his pork as if he doesn't care one way or the other.

"I can still help out around here," I say.

"Did you buy a turquoise rock yet?"

"Linus," I say.

"I don't run a boarding house, New York."

Gus wanders into the kitchen and starts sniffing at my leg. Linus tears off a hunk of meat and holds it out for him. He scratches Gus's ears, which just burns me up for some reason.

"To be clear," I say, "you don't have a daughter, right?"

He stops petting Gus. "To be clear," he says, "you did drop the hammer on your wife's cousin, right?"

And I don't answer that just the way he won't answer about his made-up daughter. I don't owe him an explanation just the same as he doesn't owe me one, I guess. I bet if you were sick the way he is and you needed help, you wouldn't want anybody heaping their pity on you, either.

So I leave in the morning, and that's the last I see of Linus Houghton. I go back to the city, but it feels different. Dirtier, more crowded. Without Karen, it feels like I don't belong so much. Like a party I wasn't exactly invited to. So I find a place way out by Yonkers. It's a crummy room in a crummy house, but it works. When I scan the *Post* each week, I still see Linus's ad, exactly the same as it was when I first saw it. *No yappy dogs.* He probably has another guy working with him now, somebody else who can split logs and won't notice he's sick for a while.

Eventually I run into you, don't I, Vick the bald museum docent? Both of you. I'm walking my side streets, nowhere else I need to be. I'm looking for our little hatchback, a note tucked in my pocket apologizing for all the hanging sausages, and there you both are, sitting on a stoop, shoulders touching, smiling. A bottle of wine on the step below you. A log of crappy, pre-packaged salami at your feet. No frowns. Like a postcard you'd buy in a gift shop.

Karen stands when she sees me. "Marty," she says.

And then you stand up, too, don't you, Vick? You aren't so bald as I thought you'd be. It's mostly just your forehead, and your hair is dark still. You're thin and have a strong jawline that I can even see through your trimmed beard. Younger than I expected, too. I'm not standing close enough, but I suspect you smell like Sean Connery would.

We stand there, awkward for a minute. Gus runs up the stoop and starts nuzzling on Karen. Then you say, "Martin. Would you care for a glass of Pinot?"

"No," I say.

"Are you certain?"

"Err, okay. Sure." Really, I just want him to stop with the talking.

You stand an extra beat, look at us both, then go inside, which seems like a classy move at the time, Vick.

I look at Karen. She seems thinner somehow. More fit. I think she dyed her hair too, some shade of brownish-black. Auburn, maybe.

"You said I was like Lopakhin," I say, though I'm pretty sure I pronounce it wrong.

"Marty," she says, "you can't be here."

"Relax," I say. "I'm not going to pelt him with bratwursts."

"You need to leave," she says. "Right now."

But I'm not going anywhere. I came to apologize for some things, get answers to some others. "Look," I say, "about the meat smell. I'm awful sorry about that. I could get a new job."

"That's good," she says.

"No more hanging sausages from the lamp shades. No more cold meat storage in our bedroom."

"We don't have a bedroom," she says. "The place is already in escrow."

I guess it's at this point I realize there's no getting her back. She sold our house, lives with you, doesn't think too much about me. Maybe she didn't squeeze Gus into her note after all.

We stand there quietly. Gus licks Karen's hands like they're made out of butter. She won't look at me. "About your cousin," I say. "That was inappropriate. I did the wrong thing there."

Karen just nods, doesn't look up, but just moves her head a little bit.

You come back out. You're not holding a wine glass. You stand in the doorway, your arms crossed. You clear your throat. "You did what wrong thing there, Martin?"

I kneel down and reach out for Gus. I don't look at you or Karen. "You know," I say.

"I do, Martin. I know what there is to know."

And this is hard to hear, you—a total stranger—knowing these kinds of things about me. It feels like a betrayal, makes me want to bolt and never come back. It's hard knowing that while I was off with Linus Houghton on his leper colony, Karen was here with you, telling our story, explaining all the horrible things I've done. Explaining about her cousin and how, yes, I did a bad thing there. My version probably makes it sound a bit more benign than it was, I admit.

No one says anything.

You take a step out of the doorway. "Do you have anything

else to add, Martin?" You reach into your back pocket and pull out your little stun rod.

But this only makes me angry. I take a step forward, and we have a little stare-off. "Marty," Karen says. "Marty, you need to leave."

I stand still for bit longer, and it instantly reminds me of all those silent fights Karen and I had over the years. I don't think for a second you'll actually use your little weapon on me.

I reach forward to grab Gus's collar, but I guess I move too fast because you jump forward and jam that stun rod into my forearm. And it hurts worse than any cut I've ever given myself. Burns into my skin, and I can even smell melted flesh. I yelp and reach down to cover it with my hand, but this hurts even worse.

"Vick!" Karen says.

"Dammit!" I shout, and I want to attack you, but my arm hurts too bad. I shake it out for a minute, and you glare at me like you'll hit me another time if I take a step forward. You really enjoyed that, didn't you? So I hold my good arm out for Gus, and he comes.

"Fine," I say as we reach the last step. "Enjoy your shitty grocery store salami and your city." And we leave.

You don't say anything. Karen doesn't say anything either, doesn't call after me to say goodbye. Doesn't even say goodbye to Gus. We walk down the street, in between the luxury cars and expensive brownstones, and I look down at my forearm. It's already blistering and purpled, and it'll be like that for a while. Might leave a scar, but it'll heal. I don't worry about it too much. Things will work out. I can't be a librarian or a bald museum docent, but people will always need meat. Not everyone can be one of those vegans. I'm sure I can snag a job in some deli in some crummy grocery store. No need to worry about me.

And you, bald museum docent. Vick. Do please be good to her. Take her to that little restaurant; get her the lamb fillet. Wear nice shoes and a sport coat. No flannels. Act like Lopakhin. Never stop wooing her, taking her to wine tastings and lectures. Make her sizzle with life every day. If she ever starts crying during sex, don't hesitate. Roll her over, ask her what's the matter, dear? Remind her there's no need to salvage anything, no secrets to protect, and you have all the time you need.

Praemonitus, Praemunitus

My son wants to be a cage fighter. He's seventeen, and so he knows a lot about everything, especially this. He's considered all the particulars, and he just knows he could be good at it. "There's a purity to it, Dad," he says. "Fighting is the original human sport."

I pray this will pass in a week or so, or perhaps the first time he gets punched in the nose hard enough to make his eyes spurt water and his brain swell against his skull.

His mother lives in Oregon, so it's just the two of us and has been for many years. It's perhaps true that I pushed the muscular pursuits too much when he was younger—a small engine repair class, full-bore target shooting, a survivalist weekend up north in which the guide informed me that anyone who called it "camping" was doing it wrong—but this was merely to lodge a few traces of grit under his fingernails, perhaps help him with the gaggle of bullies that always seem to circle him.

When none of this seemed to work, I enrolled us in a Tae Kwon Do class. I thought a martial art might help us bond, maybe give him more confidence. Toughness. But our instructor, a twenty-something kid from Colorado, smelled more like reefer than sweat and couldn't even remember Jared's name after two years. But that was my fault, trusting a Scotch Irish guy to teach Jared. White people can knock out crossword puzzles, and we make a terrific green bean casserole, but we shouldn't be teaching martial arts.

So last year I signed Jared up for wrestling at the high school, but he rarely even dresses for meets. He's too lanky, too much surface area to grab onto, all arms and legs and no torso. Horrible posture. A chest so concave you could eat soup from it. His singlet appears to be eating him. He never complains about how his teammates pick on him, but I hear them laugh about it. They throw his shoes up into the gymnasium rafters, his jock strap into the unflushed urinals. They stand too close in the showers after practice and pee on his leg while he makes shampoo mohawks.

This is the son who suddenly wants to represent the family in the cage-fighting world. I'm terrified. You spend your life toughening your kid up, hoping to give him some calluses, but then he takes it too far. Trusts your encouragement too much. This can't happen, you think. Not this. Not my kid. I have a college degree, a mortgage, a job that requires a collared shirt. I never thought I was such a bad parent that my kid would grow up and get inside a cage and kick people in the face. Don't let your kids become cage fighters or strippers: it's a universal ambition.

Jared leads me into the living room, taking his long, loping strides. I worry that I could draw an anatomically correct stick figure of him. "Watch this," he says.

He walks me through one of the cage fights on the television. Both men seem like they're still wearing shirts because they have such heavy tattoos. One of the guys sports a red mohawk, the other a shaved head. They dance around each other for a while. The crowd starts to boo. Then Shaved Head tackles Mohawk, and they tumble into the cage, which holds firm and keeps them from tumbling into the crowd. Shaved Head works on Mohawk's knees, trying to straighten them out and pin him down. He punches Mohawk's body twice, then his head, which Jared says is called "softening him up." If I didn't know any better, I'd think Shaved Head was trying to penetrate Mohawk.

"He's in half guard right now," Jared says of Shaved Head. "He's trying to get the mount, which takes the other's guys legs out of the equation. If you get the mount on a guy, you can pound his face into ground beef."

I've never heard my son talk like this.

"See how he uses the cage?" Jared says. "It's not just a barrier; they know how to use it. Just another tool in the arsenal."

Mohawk is cut under his eye, but he doesn't seem to notice. He tries to elbow Shaved Head from his back, and a few get through. One catches him on the nose, and it starts to pour blood all over them both. The announcers go ballistic, and so does the crowd.

There's under a minute left in the round, and Shaved Head turns it on. He starts dropping elbows of his own. He's dripping blood all over Mohawk's face. One of the announcers says it looks like Shaved Head is trying to end the fight before the doctors step in and stop it. It's nice to know they have doctors in the vicinity.

Shaved Head straddles Mohawk, pinning him to the mat, and Jared jumps up. "Got him!" he shouts. He's punching straight down onto Mohawk's head, jamming it into the canvas, where it ricochets just in time to get pounded again. These are big punches, and they're connecting. The crowd cheers. It reminds me of something from the *Discovery Channel*—a hyena trying to eat a baby kangaroo, perhaps. But then Mohawk pops his hips up and slides between Shaved Head's legs. "He's escaping out the back door!" the announcer shouts. Shaved Head tries to fall on him, but Mohawk swivels on his butt. He drops his legs over Shaved Head's neck and chest, grabs an arm and yanks the shit out of it, and then the ref is on top of them. The crowd completely detonates. Everyone is screaming. Jared too is standing on his toes with his arms raised. I'm not totally sure what I just saw. Mohawk, who's dripping with his own blood, won somehow. Jared tells me he dropped an armbar on Shaved Head.

"Holy shit!" I say because the little mohawked guy is a real-life ninja.

"It's called Brazilian jiu-jitsu," Jared says. "Its strength is when you're on your back and someone is on top of you."

I like the sound of that, a more defensive art form. Jared needs that.

I don't remember standing up, but I am. I'm breathing hard, and there's sweat beaded on my forehead. It's a strange and brutal sport, I think, one that awakens those contradictions that drive the hordes: the primeval lust for violence and the hope that we might tame it by locking it in a cage. And I admit that at that moment, I am one among the horde.

When I tell Jared that I'm pulling him from wrestling and putting him in Brazilian jiu-jitsu, he grins like it was his idea. He knows he's a crummy wrestler, so he needs to learn how to fight off his back. All the successful fighters can. I do my homework. Lots of them study Muay Thai. A few karate fighters but not many. Everyone agrees that you shouldn't be studying Tae Kwon Do or Kung Fu if you don't eat peanut butter and jelly sandwiches or make shitty Hollywood movies.

Jared takes to the jiu-jitsu easily. He's a quick study, his instructor says. All legs and arms, and when he learns to use them properly, they'll act like a shield for his body. Within a year, he boasts, Jared will bend his appendages like rope around his opponents. His arms will be nooses, his legs boa constrictors.

His instructor is a Brazilian about my age. Thiago Rodrigo Pereira. He's from Curitiba, which is where his family still lives, and he has a heavy Portuguese accent. Ears so cauliflowered they look like big heaping boogers clinging to his head. He's fought all over the world and could clearly beat me up and ride a unicycle at the same time. But he's an incredibly calm man, stub-legged and full of little wisdoms: *An opponent's hips are gateways to success or defeat in fighting,* he says. Or, *Look at man's eyes when first time you punch, and you see if he's been punched this way before.* One of his maxims has something to do with the fiery soul of an iguana, and I can't make sense of it. He runs a mixed martial arts center in town, one that focuses mainly on his form of jiu-jitsu. His gym, which is tucked in between a Dollar General and a KinderCare, even has a full-size steel cage for sparring. The place reeks of armpit.

"I'm all for toughening Jared up," I tell him. "But this cage fighting, I can't see him succeeding in it."

Thiago nods slowly. "I understand this," he says. "And you are right for worry. But humans are fighting. The more we practice, the more deathly we become."

"But should we encourage him?" I ask. "Do we need him getting punched in the spine?"

"No," he says very plainly. "But he will find other ways then. Humans do violence. Is natural way of things. I feel better with cages over them. Cages are for protections. Cages are good. Safer than parking lots. Better to give instructions than let them do weapons on each other."

Then I ask him if, perhaps, there is a cultural divide with fighting.

Thiago looks puzzled, and I can't tell if he's offended or working out the translation.

"It just seems," I say, "that many of these fighters are from South America or Asia."

"Ah," Thiago says. He nods. "Cultural divide. Yes."

"Then you agree?"

"No, my friend. All people fight." He stands up as if to signal his seriousness. "Forgive me," he says. "Who are best fighters of all?"

I don't know, and I fear offending him by suggesting the wrong group. "The Japanese?" I say. "The Chinese? Your Brazilians?"

"No, no," he says. "We are good fighters, but we are not best. This was Romans."

Thiago lowers his head, bowing to me. "Praemonitus, praemunitus," he says. "Forewarned is forearmed. Best prepared fighter wins victory. Romans were always best prepared."

I think the Visigoths might disagree with his assessment, but I understand his point.

"If your son prepares best, he will win victory," Thiago says. He claps me on the shoulder. "You will feel proud."

Jared sticks with the jiu-jitsu. If he's going to do this, I want him prepared. It's not uncommon, Thiago tells me privately, to have kids his age come in and claim they want to become cage fighters. Almost none of them end up doing it. I don't know if he tells me this as encouragement or consolation.

Jared advances quickly, working ten hours a week with Thiago. They roll on the mat, Thiago shouting commands about hips and wrists and posture. "Elbows in!" he shouts often, and Jared seems to struggle with this because his arms are so long. "No give up wrists!" he shouts when Jared tries to block punches. "Pancake!" he shouts when Jared gets the top position, and my son flattens out, squishing Thiago into the mat.

At home, he shows me what he learns, practicing moves on me: rear naked chokes, triangle chokes, armbars, kneebars, legbars, omoplatas, Kimuras. We move the couch and grapple each other in a Greco-Roman clinch. He slides his long arms down my chest and wraps them around my armpits, twists his hips, and chucks me to floor. He lies on the carpet and pulls me on top of him to practice his guard, wrapping his legs around my torso while I mimic punches.

"He is improving rapidly," Thiago tells me. "We must prepare more full."

I remind him that Jared already has two years of Tae Kwon Do. He looks away and grins. "Tae Kwon Do-*not*," he says, shaking his head. "This one is, like you say, very Fisher Price."

He assigns Jared a striking coach, which I have to pay extra for. He teaches Jared to keep his hands high, bounces his lead knee to block kicks. He learns basic stances to complement what he learned from the hippie Tae Kwon Do instructor: orthodox, south-paw, semi-crouch, Muay Thai. His reach is impressive—nearly that of a light-heavyweight—but his fists still seem to crumple like papier-mâché nuggets whenever they land.

He works his leg kicks on me and drives his shin bone into the meat of my thigh, and pain ripples over my whole leg like a sonic boom. I limp for two days. In the shower, I stare at the purpled bruise, push on it to feel again the newfound power of my son. Thiago is correct: I feel proud.

I pull the Acura from the garage and lay wrestling mats on the concrete slab. On the wall I stick a length of duct tape and write on it: *Praemunitus, praemonitus.* Thiago starts making house calls, and when he sees this, he scolds me. "You get them flip-side, my friend," he says. "Is not 'forearmed is forewarned.'" He shakes his head, steps on to the mat, and tries to tackle my son. I feel like a blundering, stupid American, and so I draw an arrow to signal the order needs to be switched.

Before I even realized it's happened, Thiago becomes a fixture at our house, eating dinner with us, sometimes drinking gin with me until late, when Jared is already in bed. More than once, he stays over in the guest bedroom, and they roll on the garage mats before school. His family is in Brazil; my ex-wife is in Oregon. We meet new people, use them to putty over the holes in our families.

I show him my bruised thigh one night when I've had too much to drink. He smiles broadly. "Jared is spirited fighter," he says. "You raise him well. You feel pride, yes?"

I look down and drink more gin and nod.

In early November, Jared dislocates his knee. He writhes on the mat, moaning. His face burns red as we race him to the hospital. Thiago and I stay in the waiting room while the doctor resets it. I pace back and forth, and he sits still, legs crossed.

"He will be a-okay with time, my friend," Thiago says. "This happens to me many times."

"You've convinced him he can really fight."

"Progressions are slow," Thiago says. "This confidence is important."

"And if it's misguided?" I ask. "He's six-four and 156 pounds. Jiu-jitsu doesn't change that, but he thinks it does."

It reminds of being a little boy myself, and my parents fighting over my first pellet gun. I was nine, and new people moved next door. They hitched bird feeders to everything: trees, benches, mailboxes, street lamps. If it wasn't a human or currently on fire, they fastened a bird feeder to it. Apparently the man was an ornithologist. It was still cold then, so there weren't flocks of birds, but my father didn't want to risk it. He bought me a pellet gun without talking to my mother.

"Just in case," he said to her. He didn't want to spend his evenings scraping pigeon shit off his grill.

"You're a blockhead," my mother said. "You give him a gun because we *might* develop a pigeon problem? Once the kid has the gun, I promise he'll discover a pigeon problem."

Thiago shakes his head to this. "No, no," he says. "Post hoc, ergo propter hoc. After, therefore because. Your mother believes you will kill the pigeons because you have a gun, but this is not true."

I stare at him.

"You will kill the pigeons," Thiago says, "because you are a nine-year-old boy."

And I suppose he's right. I did kill pigeons, dozens of them, and long after the bird feeder people moved away.

The doctor approaches us both and tells us it was a bad dislocation, and there is also some ligament damage. He needs to keep weight off of it for several weeks. "How exactly did it happen?" he asks.

"He fell off the roof," I say. "We were patching some shingles."

"In November?" he says and looks at Thiago. "Nothing dangerous for a while, gentlemen."

Jared limps on crutches, never complaining. He's a different kid than he used to be. He sits on the couch and shadowboxes while watching old fights. He shouts into the kitchen that his dinners need more protein in them. He does upper body and core workouts. He grows a patchy beard. He heals slowly.

By Thanksgiving, he's upright again. Thiago shows up that

evening to roll on the mat with Jared, but we give him the night off. He stays for dinner, sitting across from me in my ex-wife's former chair.

He finds Thanksgiving to be an odd holiday. "This one is for celebrate your good relations with Indians?" he asks, and I tell him that's correct.

He shakes his head. "Americans," he says and then eats a heaping pile of stuffing and green beans. Over crummy, store-bought pumpkin pie, he suggests a full-contact sparring session now that Jared is healed. "Is the next step," he says. He believes Jared is ready to face another student.

"Full-contact?" Jared says.

Thiago nods. "In the cage, full rounds, no headgear." He clearly has not considered that someone could be nervous for a fight. For Thiago, a fight is one item on an agenda: buy facial tissues, get oil change, punch people in the brain.

Jared looks over at me and nods. "This is good," he says.

It's odd, the sensation this gives me. A strange combination of embarrassment and mortification and pride.

Jared turns eighteen, and I buy three tickets to a cage-fighting event in Detroit. "Midwest Cage Fighting Touring Promotions?" he asks, reading the ticket. "Way to go all out, Dad." I realize this promotion isn't the most prestigious, kind of like watching a minor league baseball game with the Battle Creek Opossums. It's an amateur promotion. An open-mic night for fledgling ninjas.

We take Thiago along, all riding together like some new-age family en route to the local buffet. I ask Thiago about his own family, realizing I never have, and he tells us that he has not seen them for seven years. He looks out the window at the passing city lights. "My wife," he says, "she dislikes my fighting. Says I spend so much times on my back, I should be prostitute." He pauses. "My sons soldier for drug cartels," he says.

I turn and look at him. He shrugs. "Is all fighting," he says. "No cages for my boys, though."

I don't know what to say to this. We ride in silence the rest of the way, but I keep picturing Thiago's boys, camouflaged in the wilderness, searching for rival drug mules, shouldering their AK-47s, shouting commands and then pointing their guns at anything that moves too quickly.

We sit cage-side in what seems to be a junior high gymnasium. I enjoy the fighter introductions, especially the nicknames, so menacing they're comical: Brent "The Kalamazoo Wolverine" Carlson; "Vodka" Joe Nemerov; Jonah "Rigor Mortis" Morris. I tell Jared his new nickname is "Giraffe," but he finds this less funny than I do. In fact, he looks tense sitting this close. He leans back on his seat, as if it is an electric fence he must never touch.

The main event is a lightweight match—Jared's division—between a local kid with no nickname who wears glasses to the ring and looks like he came directly from biology class and "Vodka" Joe Nemerov. Vodka Joe couldn't possibly look more Russian if he bench-pressed Lenin's embalmed body in the middle of Red Square. His widow's peak descends between his eyes like an arrowhead, and he grimaces for no apparent reason. I suspect his solution to a broken clavicle would involve rubbing bear fat on it. His eyes bulge and do not leave Dr. Biology.

Dr. Biology is outclassed. The program tells us he holds a black belt in jiu-jitsu, but it seems hard for him to enact any defense or submission while he's getting punched in the head. Vodka Joe thumps his face so many times, it swells tight and goes tomato red. His cheeks puff inward, as if trying to pinch his nose. An elbow slices above his eye, leaving a canyon of a gash. By the end of the first round, Dr. Biology is a limping, bleeding pile of loss.

In the second round, Vodka Joe pins him up against the fence directly in front of us. He punches down, drops elbows onto Dr. Biology's head again and again, like enormous pistons reciprocating in their cylinders. Dr. Biology can't move—the cage curls him up in an awkward position—and we hear him moan, long, guttural whimpers like some pathetic animal in the process of becoming roadkill. I stand up, lean toward the cage for better angle, and when I do, Vodka Joe drops a stiff right cross onto the kid's mouth, loosing gobs of thick blood and spittle through the cage and onto my jacket. I breathe it in, the blood and sweat, and I briefly think that I could do this, that its base is pure violence, not martial arts. I could pound other men in the head, slice down with elbows. These men should feel lucky that they have a cage guarding them from me.

The referee finally steps in and waves his arms, and Vodka Joe starts celebrating. Dr. Biology sits against the cage like a tree stump. I turn back to see Jared wiping splattered blood from his brow. He isn't looking at me, isn't looking at the cage. He gazes down, taking long breaths. Sitting cage-side is new to him. Blood is new to him. Thiago sits next to him, legs crossed and calm, as if he has just listened to a panel of blue hairs talk about doilies and denture cream.

No one talks during the drive home. Jared says good night very quietly and closes his bedroom door. I examine myself in the mirror and realize I've somehow missed a dried speck of Dr. Biology's blood that must have splashed me. I lean in close and scratch it off.

I lie on the couch and picture the fight. I can't ignore how badly I wanted to jump in there and help, tear through the cage and kick the poor kid like Vodka Joe, like my next meal depended on it. The damage I could have done. I'm suddenly a hunter, a ferocious brute of a man, a shirtless Roman stomping into the Flavian Amphitheater to dispatch all living things. Thiago is right: humans are fighters. We're a violent and successful species. We didn't rise to the top of the food chain by baking muffins for our predators. We did it by making them our prey. And now that all our natural predators gone, now that we've conquered them and erected mini-malls in their old habitats, we turn toward one another because what every species covets is an enemy.

Jared's sparring opponent is no kid. He's an older man, mid-thirties perhaps, with bad teeth and mangy hair that looks like mulch.

He's built like a 155-pound midget-lumberjack, as wide as he is tall, his neck seeming to sprout directly from his ass. He has an eye tattooed on the back of his neck, and I know immediately my son is in trouble.

I stand cage-side. I stare at Jared as he stretches his long limbs and pulls on the fingerless five-ounce gloves. He windmills his arms, bounces on the balls of his feet. He hangs from the cage top, and each vertebra pops as his spine lengthens. Thiago calls them to center of the ring and reminds them of the rules, reminds them it is full-contact, long rounds, standard stoppages for strikes and submissions. "Real fight, gentlemen," he says.

Jared wilts almost immediately. Lumberjack makes no attempt to strike with him. Thiago tells them to fight, and he rushes at my son, closes the distance before Jared even has his feet set. Jared topples over, and Lumberjack straddles him, axing the point of his elbow into Jared's ribs. Then to his sternum, then his jaw. Jared flails from the bottom, his legs fluttering as if he might gather enough lift to fly away if only he keeps gesticulating.

I'm not at all prepared for this. My muscles clench, and I shout to him, shout angry nothings about relaxing and wrist control. All the things I've heard Thiago scold into him. Jared hears none of my pleas—this I can tell. His eyes widen, and he's forgotten where he is, can't feel the mat below him or see Thiago above, looking down with his sad eyes. He's in an alley, behind a dumpster, writhing on a heap of cracked asphalt and gutter juice. And this hulking savage aims to cannibalize him. Jiu-jitsu no longer exists. His legs are garter snakes, not boa constrictors. This fight is as righteous as mine was with the pigeons.

Lumberjack flattens Jared out, cranks on his neck, and punches on his temple. Jared yelps. He tries to grab Lumberjack's wrist but gets shaken off. He's a buoy with no jurisdiction over movement, just wobbling along with the currents that Lumberjack spews.

"Defend yourself!" Thiago shouts to Jared. "Intelligent defense."

Jared bleeds from the corner of his eye. Lumberjack has gashed one cheek open and notched a dent into his forehead. I can see the blood pooling there.

I grip the cage harder. I shake it. I clutch it and tear my hands near-bloody until it seems the beaded steel will decapitate my fingertips. I feel that primal ache loose from me, and I want nothing more than to rip my way through the stockade. To chew through the steel ropes if I must and enter that place where I would stomp through Thiago and fall to my knees and hammer on Lumberjack's spine with my heavy Neanderthal fists until all his breath left him. And when I turned to my bleeding son, he would most certainly recognize me as his father, as that most savage of all predators.

But there I stand, my hands on the fence, my pink fingers wrapping around the links, the cage guarding its fighters like the last lonely sentinel of our civilization.

Patriots

Here's a story what got passed around from some folks I gone to school with down in Hocking County. You got these two cousins called Harlow and Tuber who light out from Ohio thinking to deal with the Vietcong but end up pretty well dealt with instead. Harlow, he was a mouthy little balker, like some yappy blue jay. Tuber was the fighting type, looked an awful lot like a potato, which everyone was always telling him. Tuber was put together strange if you're asking me, squished up, like that kind of midget who's okay on thickness but not on length. He was regular size enough what the army took him, but since he was so small, he ended up a tunnel rat, and Christ knows what awful shit he done and seen.

Both these boys go and enlist, and it's Harlow what decides he needs a tattoo. Harlow was like that, couldn't do good without making it a scene or bad without trying to convince you it was good. Always talking, Harlow. Tuber says he'll go along, thinking Harlow don't have the brass to go through with it. They borrow somebody's truck and drive way over to this tattoo parlor in Lancaster. They're looking at all the options plastered up on the wall, a thousand of them, more maybe, Harlow talking all the way: *This one here might be right* and *You imagine the cooch a guy like me'd pull with this one?* and *Even you'd seem a tough son of a bitch with this one, Tube.*

Here, I imagine the old fella what owns the tattoo shop shaking his head at Harlow and Tuber, them being a big bucketful of stupid. Course a guy like that probably needs stupid teenagers to make his business work out. Harlow finally settles on one, a bald eagle with an American flag hanging from its feet. Patriotic as all hell. That's what the story is, course he don't end up getting that one because right about then a couple old bikers walk in, leather vests, no shirts underneath, skin like old farmhouse floorboards, facial hair stained with chaw drip. What's wrong, though, what Harlow and Tuber and the old tattoo fella should have picked out, is that these two don't have no tattoos.

"How's things, friend?" the first one says. He strolls around, not really looking at anyone, more like sizing the place up to buy it. The other one, he's a big bruiser, stands in front of the door and don't say much. No way he's letting Harlow and Tuber get by, that much is easy to see.

The old fella what runs the place is looking a little nervous now. One of them times you can just tell shit's heading south quick, them two's not the kind you want to be alone with. Not the kind of thing he put in for. But he holds it together and says, "Just fine now. What might we be doing for you all today?"

The first biker, the leader, he keeps strolling around the edges of the shop same as Harlow and Tuber was a few minutes before. He's looking at all the tattoos. His boots strike on the laminate, and when they do, his wallet chain jangles. He stops when he notices Tuber. "The hell, son? Your folks run out of food or what?"

That's normally enough to get Tuber all up and bothered, but he just says, "No, sir. I eat okay."

The biker walks over toward him. "I'd make you for the king dick-sucker of this town," he says. "Don't even need to squat down." Then he laughs at his own joke and looks over to his partner, who grins but don't laugh.

"Well, we ain't even from this town," Harlow says.

The biker looks over to Harlow and studies on him a minute. "Oh, so you're the smart one, huh? I can always tell the smart one. Gift I got." He takes a step over toward him. "Okay, smart one, how smart do you feel now?" He pulls out a flick blade and it jumps open. Then his big partner does the same.

"Oh, now!" the old fella what runs the place says. "No need for that, gentlemen. We don't want no trouble. Ain't got but a few dollars on hand, but you're welcome to those."

"You hear that, Hopper?" the first biker says. "Think we're here to rob them out."

"That's what they usually think," Hopper says. His voice is deeper but quieter than his friend's, like he can't be bothered to care about too much.

"No, sir," the main biker says, "Not here to rob you. Here for a tattoo."

"That we can do, sir. No need for that knife then."

"You're right, ain'tcha?" He closes the blade and stuffs it in his front pocket. "I'll just leave it right here, right in this front pocket, so we don't forget about it, huh? Now, back to this tattoo. I don't see it nowhere, not what I'm looking for," he says.

"I can do whatever you like. Just tell me, and I'll draw it up."

"Now that's the spirit!" The biker grabs a marker from next to the cash register. He goes over to the wall and finds the one empty spot in between all the other sample tattoos. Got his back to Harlow and Tuber and the old fella, so they can't see what he's drawing till after he's done, but it don't take him long, and when he moves away, it's a big black swastika he drew. No mistaking it. "Now, I ain't the artist I'm betting you are," he says, "but that's the rough cut of it."

"Sir," the old tattoo fella says, but Christ, what's he supposed to do? It's like he knows he's fucked deep, but he can't just go on and do it without complaining some. Folks have swastika tattoos, I guess, but it don't seem right what they make somebody else draw it on them. But the old fella says, "Okay, then, go ahead and set down in that chair and I'll get things ready."

"Oh, it ain't for me," the biker says. "I don't care for tattoos, myself. Ruin my complexion." He runs a hand through his beard.

"No, I want it for this one here, the smart one." He points at Harlow.

"Sir—"

"Now, friend," he says, "let's not get on repeating ourselves. We know what's in the front pocket, and we know what I want, so let's just get on with it."

The old tattoo fella's all jammed up, no doubt about that. He looks over at Harlow, his face drooping like a hungry dog, probably trying to apologize a thousand different ways without saying nothing out loud. But then Harlow, to that boy's credit, he rips his shirt off, his ribcage poking through his skin, and he walks over to the chair and sets on down.

"Goddamn, if I wasn't right!" the biker says. "You are smart."

The old tattoo man sets things up and goes to work, and it don't take him but half an hour to mark Harlow up with the swastika. It's thick and dark, and it covers up the whole left side of his chest. Harlow, he don't make a goddamned sound, that's the story I heard anyways. His whole life he's been the loudmouth, always telling folks how he'd do this or he'd do that, how he pulls so much cooch that don't even get the clap no more, how he's the toughest son of a bitch around, but right then he just takes it, quiet and almost dignified. "Damn, son," the biker says, "that can't feel good now." But Harlow don't say boo, and the old biker don't push it like he done before.

That's the end of the story as most people in town learned it, but there's more to it I heard years later when I came back to the states for a reunion and I run into Harlow's sister. I was always sweet on her but never had the stones to talk to her until after I was safe and married. Turns out Harlow and Tuber head off to basic a couple months later and then over to Vietnam a couple months after that. They end up in different units, but they try to talk when they can. It's Tuber what makes a real show of himself as a tunnel rat. I guess he's just fearless, like he knows he was engineered just for it. Got a whole process. Every hole and bunker they come across, Tuber strips down to his skivvies and takes just a flashlight and a .45. Sometimes he's gone a long time, but he eventually comes back and calls it clear, meaning there wasn't nothing down there or there was but now there ain't. Then he packs the hole with explosives and they set off. Tuber earns medals and commendations and all that. Harlow's sister tells me all about it, like she remembers all the details all these years after, which seems strange, but I guess ain't seeing as what Tuber done for her brother next.

It's Harlow what dies first, takes one from a sniper outside Kien Long. Here's the part what really sticks to me, though. Harlow gets shipped back stateside to get buried back in Ohio, and when Tuber hears about all this he loses it. His CO won't give him leave, not even after everything he done in them tunnels, not even for his cousin being dead, his cousin who was Tuber's best friend. So Tuber goes AWOL. Somehow he manages to get back stateside, and the night before Harlow's funeral, he breaks into the funeral parlor, jamming that .45 into the mortician's temple. "I'm needing you to do this on the pronto," Tuber says to him, and the mortician don't do much for protest. He sets Harlow's body up on the table and helps Tuber strip him out of his new suit, all so Tuber can take a razor blade to his cousin's chest and carve out that swastika, seeing as I guess he couldn't stand the thought of him getting buried with that still there.

The cops show up, and he don't make no big scene out of it. He goes quiet, even gives the mortician his .45, like he knew it was coming. Turns out it weren't even loaded. He gets charged with carving up a corpse and burglary and assault, which sends him inside for a few years. Worst part? Army finds out he gone AWOL and broke into the funeral home, they discharge him too, dishonorable after all he done. Harlow's sister says Tuber gets the final papers his first week inside. "Did you write him? I ask, and she says, "Yeah, I wrote him most every week," which is what I was hoping for.

"That's good," I say. "You always was a good sister."

I lean in a little closer so we can whisper through the loud music. I set my drink next to hers, rims almost touching. That's when she looks at me pretty mean, and I know what's coming, I been waiting on it. "How long you lived in Windsor anyway?"

"Long time now," I say, and when she don't respond, I say, "You know how things was."

"Yeah," she says. "I guess I do."

We chat about the old days for a few more minutes, and then she says she needs to go to the bathroom, and I don't see her after that. It's funny what you remember and what you tell people about. Always seems like you end up telling the wrong stories or telling the right stories the wrong way. Never can seem to get it right, and besides, nobody ever hears you all the way through anyhow.

The Dogs of Detroit

Nights, when Polk cannot hunt the dogs, he instead attacks his father. He has grown to crave the hot pain spreading over his face, the bulging of his knuckles when they connect with bone. His father fights back just enough. They roll around on the floor, struggling and grunting, sneaking in shots to the ribs and the temples. When they tire, they each collapse, wheezing, moaning. They rub their flushed faces and lick away the blood pooling on their gums and retreat to their corners. No resentment or words, as if they are not punching each other, not exactly. A narcotic hunger being fed, one which brings no joy but rather is a conduit for torment.

After their fights they lay there, panting, blinking back tears, and only then does Polk confide in his father. He lists off the revenges he wants to take on the universe. He imagines the worst things possible: toddler coffins, flayed penguins, pipe bombs in convents, napalm in orphanages. He hates himself for it, his selfishness, his appetite for sloppy justice. Always he ends up wondering the same thing: *Does God hate me more than I hate God?*

His father reaches for Polk's hand, but Polk pulls away. No touching unless it is to create violence. "Patience," his father says. "We must learn grief."

After school, Polk hunts. He ranges across the urban wilderness of the East Side, ducks through the cutting winds off Saint Clair. He lugs a Winchester bolt action by the barrel, dragging the stock on the ground, leaving a crease in the snow. He tracks dog prints through the industrial fields, through the brambled grasses and split concrete and begrimed snow. Through decomposing warehouses and manufacturing cathedrals which nature has reclaimed. Hundreds of deserted acres. These are wild dogs he kills, no longer bear any trace of domestication. Few people left, but the dogs—thousands of dogs, abandoned during this great human exodus. There is no Atticus Finch to blast the rabies from them, no little girl to drag them home by the scruff to her father and say *May we please?* As all else crumbles, the dogs remain.

And then one day: his mother's tracks, long and narrow, weight on the outside ridges. Keds. She always wore Keds. She has been gone two months now, disappeared. She was there when Polk went to school, sitting at the kitchen table, sucking on a menthol, gone when he got home. But these are her prints. He knows them. They mix in with the dog prints, as if she has joined them. Perhaps has been hunted by them, perhaps something else altogether.

Eventually, he thinks, *I'll whiten the canvas, leaving only her tracks. Eventually, a pattern will emerge.* But with each dog he kills, his palate mutates: joy. The heavy thunk of bullet piercing a ribcage. Eliminating a contagion. A growing pleasure to be found in mindless violence. Carcasses left to rot, to ravage by predators. Always there seem to be more dogs, like a muscle in need of constant stretching.

At school, he sits alone. He is a large boy, the largest in the junior high school, his feet flapping on the concrete hallways as if they were made for an adult but then attached to him instead. The art teacher, Mrs. Roudebush, prods him to rejoin the world. More pictures of mom, Polk? More charcoal? Why not try the acrylics? Some greens and yellows and magentas.

"No, thank you," he says. His face remains placid, all its topography flattened, grown numb, unable to flex. He refuses to look up, and she soon wanders away to check on other students.

After school, he walks home to their house on the East Side, then through the tunnel of tall grasses, which have swallowed up all but the second story where they never go. Collapsed staircase, plywood windows, a contentedness in allowing it to erode.

These winter days the sun never truly rises. No direct light, no marbled streaks or roiling clouds, just a vast gray slab. Slowly, the night mottles into blued steel as if other colors have not yet been discovered. He grabs the Winchester and sets off, follows the freshest of the dog prints as far as they will take him, across the freeway and toward the old Packard compound, its remnants. He nestles onto a hillside, his favorite perch, downwind. A sniper in Stalingrad. He takes down two dogs quickly, the echoes of the rifle shots ballooning around out in waves. The sun droops. A mangy pit bull trots into the field, and Polk takes it down, the round ripping through the dog back near its haunches, and it stumbles, tries to limp away, dragging its paralyzed legs. For several minutes it struggles forward, and Polk watches. Then it stops moving. Polk trudges home, stomping wide holes in the snow, the butt of the Winchester digging a crease behind him. His mother's prints, which had been clear the day before, have vanished, taken by the wind.

Mrs. Roudebush introduces tertiary colors: chartreuse, magenta, russet, azure. "These," she says, "are the gems. The true colors of nature. Turned leaves are not red or yellow or pink. They are citron, plum, vermilion."

"Hey, *Poke*," one boy with shaggy hair and an earring whispers across the table. "Hey, mamma's boy." Polk used to know the boy's name, but he has forgotten it. Usually, they leave him alone, but sometimes he is such easy prey they seem not to be able to help themselves.

The kids at his table whisper just loudly enough that he can hear. "His mom used to smoke crack," a girl says.

"I know it," another girl says. "I seen her do it with my stepdad."

"Poke likes crack too, don't you, Poke?" The boy leans across the table, but just then Mrs. Roudebush kneels next to Polk.

"This is one of my favorites," she whispers. She hands him a tube of paint. "Viridian. I wonder if you might try it today."

Polk feels that this lesson is designed specifically for him. Adults talk differently after tragedy, as if he is suddenly six years old rather than thirteen. He paints a picture of his mother at the kitchen table. The tip of her cigarette is viridian, the smoke coiling off is slate. Her hair is russet, the table is buff. The clock on the wall, which is actually yellow, he decides to paint plum so that it barely distinguishes itself. He catches the shadows with gray-browns and blue-grays, and before long the scene emerges from his memory, protrudes through the paper like a hologram.

He paints her teeth, paints the spaces between them, wide enough for a pencil point. Her rotting gums are some mix of gray and brown, like frozen mud. Her foggy eyes tired, unable to focus. Her head rocking as if to some silent melody. He paints his father standing in the doorway, arms crossed. He is half looking at her, half looking at the floor, as if he cannot decide which is more painful.

"Fetch your mother a Diet," she says to Polk, and he does. It's warm. Broken refrigerator. She tries to light another menthol, but she shakes too badly. She puts her elbows on the table, leans down toward the lighter. Polk watches her struggle and fail, and then he snatches the lighter, bends down, and lights the cigarette for her.

"You love you mother, don't you, Polk?"

"Marie," Polk's father says. They stare at each other.

"I know it," she says. "Tomorrow."

"Time for school," his father says, reaching for him, drawing him away from the kitchen, out the front door. What he remembers now is that he never answered her question—*You love your mother, don't you, Polk*? He went to school instead. *Yes*, he should have said. *Even like this.*

That afternoon she vanished.

Polk's father is waiting for him on the front sidewalk. Polk tries to sidestep him and go in the house and take the Winchester and do his duty.

"Polk," his father says. "No more guns."

Polk stares blankly.

"The police called again. They're done understanding."

"Have they found her or not?" Polk asks.

"Polk, that's not—"

"I know what you think."

"You don't."

"I know you don't miss her. I know that. You never even cried."

His father sits on the top step. He won't look at Polk. "I know you feel like you're stuck with me now. I know you loved her more. I can't do anything about that."

Polk points toward the industrial complex. "I see her prints."

His father squints. "All kind of bums and druggos hide out in that place. What are you doing over there?"

Polk doesn't answer.

"You can't trust those. Those could be anything. We both knew her."

"I can tell when people think I'm lying," he says.

His father sighs and looks away. "Polk," he says but then decides not to finish. Finally, he says, "We can't keep doing this."

"You don't believe me. You never believed her either."

"Polk, I believe you."

"Don't do that."

"Polk, you need to stop this."

Something in Polk fractures. Can't compartmentalize anger and pain anymore. They bleed together. He puts his hands on his knees, tries to slow it, long breaths, closed eyes.

His father recognizes the signs. "Can it wait?"

Polk shakes his head, no, and his father nods, alright then.

They stomp through the high grass and dirty snow of the front yard, tamp down a wide circle that feels like a cage. Polk tackles his father but can't bring him down. He yanks and twists a leg, secures it under his armpit until his father finally goes down, knees to the snow. They're trundling around then, back and forth like a rolling pin, neither gaining position. Polk takes an elbow to the sternum, which knocks his breath loose, and he rolls to his back. He kicks up, punches, his father smacking his face raw and red. Polk feels the meat of his fist half connect with something but doesn't know what. White noise and blur. His nose gets mashed, and the tears come then, no stopping it. He bucks, loosing the last bit of his anger, exploding up, pivoting at his hips, and driving his father down, then hammering his fists into chest. He clasps his fists together and churns his arms down like a piston, boring his way down onto his father.

And then it's over. No more energy, no more anger. They exist together. For several minutes they hardly move, just pant and cough. This is the normal trajectory. Soon, they will rise to their knees, then stand and move into the house.

"Syringe Ebola into baby formula," Polk says. He's gasping, the words pulsing out in blurred waves. "Hack a newborn giraffe with a machete."

"Okay."

"Dynamite the Statue of Liberty."

"Enough now."

"Grocery bags full of puppy ears."

"Polk."

Polk stops sleeping in his bed. Too soft, too warm. Goodness to be found in small miseries: cold floors, festering splinters, fingertips burnt on light bulbs. He lies on the floorboards, no pillow, no blanket.

Outside the wind ravages the old house. The dogs, he can hear the dogs, howling and snarling, and then more snow comes, dampening the yelping echoes and covering old tracks. There is no sleep, not anymore, only an untended aggression that needs fed.

She is near, he knows this. He begins smelling her perfume, flowers and vanilla. More than once he moves her old ashtray from the table to the counter only to have it moved back by the morning. His father does not smoke. And of course, her prints. Is she too ashamed to come back? Is that it? Or is she angry with him because he didn't say he loved her?

He sees her tracks again one morning, fresh tracks in the fresh snow. Not twenty feet from the front door, pacing around the grass cage where he fought his father. Keds, very clearly Keds. They slither through the tall grass, around the north side of house, up to each of the front windows. There they shrink and push deeper into the snow. On her tiptoes, peering in. He feels her lingering presence, as if they are trying to occupy the same space, as if she is trying to make sense of what has happened since she left. He examines each print, follows them out the backyard and through the split chain links. He tracks them north, fifty yards into the fields, the longest he has ever been able to track her, but then they enter into a depression of ice and evaporate. He circles around looking for an exit point, but there is none. Gone again.

Nearby is the pit bull mix that he shot the week before. It has a distinctive brindle pattern to its coat. Dilutions of gold on a black base crawl as if trying to escape. He is exposed, vulnerable without his rifle. Its stomach has been opened up, devoured. The other dogs, hungry for whatever protein still exists in this wasteland. And he thinks for a moment of the oddity of it all, how he kills the dogs and leaves them to rot, how the other dogs eat their pack-mates to survive. He hunts them and hunts *for* them. This canvas will never whiten. He isn't sure what all this means, but he does know that the natural order of things has been upended, that he is caught up in it somehow.

Polk steals paint from school, tertiary colors, fills in every set of prints that might be hers. He squeezes paint into each print, filling it fully, cleanly, spreads it over every contour, and then moves on to the next print, and soon her trail glows, emerging from the snow and mud like collapsed stars. The paint will harden, freeze, will remain fixed there for as long as it takes for Polk to make sense of them. No more disappearing trails. He uses his stash of paints to categorize them by color, by direction, by timeframe, then draws a tape measure around the expanse of compound, slowly, from one set of prints to another, even measures stride lengths. He notes everything.

The dogs eye him but keep their distance, curiosity and mockery. Like an undertaker gazing at a body, perhaps. Polk doesn't feel hunted exactly, but he feels something at the base of his skull, their lurking curiosity, feels how little he now belongs in this place. It belongs to the dogs.

Nights, he sits at the kitchen table. He moves the ashtray with her menthol butts to the counter, begins drawing a scaled map, every feature of the area, every print of hers, every color noted. He feels like a scientist tracking the migration patterns of some near-extinct species of bird. In time, her own patterns will emerge, her location. They must. For the first time since she disappeared he feels a goodness in himself, a warmth not from violence.

"What's this?" his father asks.

"I'm not allowed to shoot the dogs anymore."

His father sits next to him, looks the map over for a moment. "These are places you've seen her trail?"

Polk nods.

"This many?"

Polk keeps drawing, tracing a pencil across a ruler. Slow, precise movements.

"Polk?" his father says quietly, but Polk ignores him. He spends all evening drawing a map of the area, each set of prints noted and appropriately colored to indicate a timetable.

"My little cartographer," his father says, but Polk ignores him still. This is more than a map. This is a timeline, a psychological study.

The next day, her ashtray is back on the table again. There are cigarettes in it, menthol butts that do not seem new but that he can't recall seeing before.

He begins to see her footprints everywhere, glowing at him. They emerge from his father's eyes. He sees them in headlights and oddly thrown shadows; during art class; in his dreams when he sleeps in short, hateful spurts. Sometimes the dog tracks morph as he stares at them, become longer, narrow, deeper on the ridges. Sometimes they are large and sometimes small, but they are all hers, this he knows.

"It's not fair," his father says. "None of it. I know that." He tries to massage Polk's shoulders, but Polk shies away. These attempts are clumsy and practiced now. They aren't a family; they're remnants of one. When she disappeared, their tripod crumbled.

There was a time, not very long ago, when they had been happy. He knows this now because he never thought about being happy. They had jobs, his father at the machine shop, his mother in the deli at the Kit Kat. She always brought home bologna that was almost expired, and they would fry it up until it bubbled and popped.

He clings to a single memory. Sledding a small scoop of a hill near baseball fields, dirty snow packed down. He tries to remember where this hill was, but the location eludes him. *Was it a false memory?* he wonders. Something he has manufactured to cope? His mother would give Polk a big shove, and he would slingshot down the hill, skittering and spinning where it turned into ice and when the speed became too much, he closed his eyes, afraid to see what lay below. Each time he shot down the hill he lost control, but always he would end up at the bottom, face up in the snow, always his father waiting, asking *Should we go again?* Then walking back to the house, having to wedge himself between his mother and his father because they were holding hands. He remembers her smell, flowers and vanilla. When they got home, he took a shower, but the water had gone cold again. Bad plumbing, dud water heater. When he walked into the front room still shivering and wet his father pulled a towel from the oven and swaddled him with it, and his skin slowly softened, his breaths lengthened until he felt whole and content.

Polk stops going to school, spends the days painting tracks, updating his map. He is meticulous, always bent over a set of prints or making notations. The pattern will emerge, the methods to her movements, this he knows. He plunges deep into the grounds of the Packard compound, even venturing into the buildings when he is feeling brave. Sometimes he sees vandals, other times photographers, but mostly he sees dogs and homeless who share the various buildings in relative peace. He maps and paints, maps and paints. He stops sleeping, just expands the map, growing weary and unpredictable. Everything begins to feel random. It begins to look like a star map, with constellations emerging, glowing at him.

One day, Polk comes home to find Mrs. Roudebush sitting at the table with his father. She clutches her purse and smiles at him, her sad smile like an apology. "We've missed you," she says.

Polk looks down, and his eyes land on his hands, his large and awkward hands smeared with paint. He looks back up at Mrs. Roudebush, but before he is forced to speak, she reaches into her purse and pulls out a paper bag. She sets it on the table. "I was doing some cleaning," she says. She stands up to leave, hangs her purse from her shoulder. "My husband," she says, "he died three years ago."

Polk feels himself flinch and stare at her.

"I used to roll over in the middle of the night, and he was in bed with me. Sometimes I even heard him snore. I swear I did. Sometimes I would wake up, and his radio would be going. I told my sister about it, but you could tell she didn't believe me. That was hard. I couldn't understand why it had to be like that. I refused to change the sheets because I thought he was in there somehow. I slept on those sheets for a year, every night hoping to feel him or smell him or hear his snores. Sometimes I did, and sometimes I didn't. It was all I thought about. I moved the microwave and the television into the bedroom. I lived in there. One day, my sister found me like that, and she made me take a shower and wash the sheets. Do you know what we found when we stripped the bed?"

Polk shakes his head, no.

"A small painting, an acrylic on canvas, no stretcher. At first I didn't recognize it, but then I realized it was a scene I had done, probably thirty years ago, not long after we were married, my husband thin and clean shaven, me thin and with a long pony tail. We were standing in front of our first house, not far from here. I had forgotten about that painting, but there it was under the mattress pad."

She looks to Polk's father. "There's no explaining that."

"Did he put it there?" Polk asks.

"I don't know, dear. I really don't. But I think the dead teach us how to grieve," she says. "I don't understand it, either, but that's what I think. Sometimes people can be gone and not gone at the same time. They know things we don't know." She smiles at him. "God doesn't hate you, Polk."

That night Polk lies on the floor. The bag of paint sits next to him. He hasn't yet opened it, but he knows what's in there. He wants to go outside right then and use them, take a flashlight and find the tracks and paint them. *What are you trying to teach me?* he wonders. He finds himself packing a bag of supplies: bottles of water, beef jerky, Skittles, dog treats, extra socks, a Maglite, toilet paper. He rolls his set of maps up tightly.

He walks out into the kitchen, where his father is sitting at the table. He turns to look at Polk, and dangling from his lips is a cigarette butt. Remnants of her. It has been stubbed out and twisted, unlit, hanging limply. His father is startled. "Polk," he says. "Can't you sleep?"

"She's out there," he says. "Every night, right now, she's out there. Her tracks are freshest in the morning."

"No," his father says. He pulls the cigarette from his mouth and delicately places it back in the ashtray as if it is some fragile treasure. "You're not doing this."

Polk shrugs. It's time, he knows this. If he waits much longer, he'll lose her.

"I've let this go on too long."

"You have to sleep at some point," Polk says.

"I won't allow this."

"I'll bring her home," Polk says.

"She's not out there, Polk. You're looking for trouble. You want to join her."

"You're just glad she's gone. You don't have to help her now."

His father smacks him then, the flat of his palm on Polk's cheek. This is by no means the first time his father has struck him, but this time is different—this is anger.

Polk pounces on this father. They tumble over the table, spill onto the floor. They struggle. Polk hears himself grunt and snarl. He doesn't punch and kick so much as he thrashes wildly. Then he catches an elbow to the eye, and the world blurs. He yelps with the pain, grabs at it with both hands. His father stops, bends over Polk to examine it.

"Let me look at it, Polk."

There is a cut clean through his eyelid, like a half-peeled orange. It won't close all the way. Even when he tries, light seeps through the crack. Everything is mottled, ill-defined edges, blurred colors. They put ice on it, then a hot rag, then some ointment. "Polk," his father says. "Jesus, Polk. I didn't—"

"It's fine. I'm fine."

"You need stitches."

"Stop." Polk wheezes and coughs. "It felt good, didn't it?"

His father looks like he is the one who is wounded. "Do you really think that?" His face is drawn, defeated. He bends and picks up the ashtray and butts and sweeps the ashes into a pile. He doesn't look up. "If you want to go, I can't stop you."

The moon glows full, or near-full, throwing an eerie sort of light, like the structures themselves blush. Polk must cock his head to the side or cover his thrashed eye to see more clearly. Soon he is trolling the site, rummaging from building to building, tracing his way methodically, following his maps. Even after months of scouting dogs, tracking his mother, noting everything, he has explored only a fraction of the compound. It is like a series of cave systems that turn out to be linked, spreading out forever in all directions. But he has supplies. He will mimic her movements for as long as it takes.

He sniffs his way through one building at a time, one floor at a time, scouring every closet, every side room, behind every pile of rubble, his flashlight flickering in every direction. Collapsed staircases and crumbling masonry and bowed walls. Drips through the open roof, frozen like milky stalactites. All abandoned, as if in haste: filing cabinet drawers thrown open like gaping maws; a '57 Clipper, no engine block, sitting mute on the line; rebar poking through split concrete; cottonwood trees growing from floorboards, leaning away from Saint Clair's wind. He shoos away dogs, passes sleeping bodies without a word. For the first time, Polk feels real fear, a coldness clenching his torso. The feeling that he is not alone, that he is the one being tracked now. Until now he didn't care what happened to him, but the vast quiet of this crypt is too terrifying, the fact that he see shapes and colors more than fully defined objects.

He soon feels that he could map this system for years and still be no nearer to finding her. All night he explores, makes notations on his maps, stoops to examine prints. Prints all over. This is a populated world, crowded with life: dogs, cats, foxes, at least one coyote. Humans. He passes them silently as they lay curled, backs to the wind. Some of them shiver, but most seem not to notice him. He is certain he hears a baby cry at one point. He stands still, waits for the cry to pierce the silence again, but there is only the long quiet, the creaking of the buildings. When he moves off there is a long and shrill howl of a dog, first a single wail, and then others respond, some far off but others nearer, too near. He twists his head to listen. Are they communicating? Pack-mates on the hunt?

Then a crawling sensation, like the shock from a nine-volt on the tongue. Then the smell: his mother's perfume, flowers and vanilla.

He spins around. No one. He narrows his eyes like an eagle, glares into every crevice of the room, tilts his flashlight at every angle, sees nothing, no one. He tilts his head, uses his good eye. Nothing. He sniffs deeply: menthols.

"Are you here?" he says. The first words he has spoken all night. Then: "Why here?"

This is when he would usually attack his father, loose that confused anger onto the world where it might dissolve. But there is no one here, no violence he can inflict. He tries to think of brutal things to do to the world, but none come to him. It is as if some awful weariness has flattened him. How long has he been here? When did he last sleep? Everything is tertiary colors pulsing from a fuzzy black background, moonlight, haze.

When he moves away from the wall, it is green moss everywhere. Where there was snow, now there is moss. Plush, spongey. Her prints stamped into it. They should be his own prints, but they are hers. The deeper trenches at the ridges, the veiny webs on the soles, the short span between each heel strike. They are hers. He follows them, careful not to trample. They lead up a grand staircase, through a series of offices, over creaking wood floors and concrete ground into gravel. Silence, all silence and the cutting reek of menthol.

He follows the trail, follows the smell. They tug him along as if he wears a belay line. Soon he is trotting, climbing upward, ignoring the stomping noise he makes, the commotion of disturbing a closed system. He emerges on the roof, a surface so vast it seems like he is back on the ground. He meanders among a grove of cottonwoods that poke through the concrete. They are leafless, their icy limbs shaking in the wind, clattering and creaking. The tang of menthol grows stronger. He coughs and has to wipe away the hot seep from his eye. He doesn't trust this, none of this. To the east, a small breech in the darkness, the sun climbing toward the horizon, the moonlight diffusing. The scent dissipates. He turns and looks behind him. No moss, only snow, pure and untouched but for his fat mashed footprints. He gazes around, everything blurry like he is under water. There is nothing here, not his mother, not even traces of her.

Another high-pitched wail, closer this time, washing over the whole rooftop. Silence for a few heartbeats. Silence. And then the response, an answer that seems to emanate from the cottonwood grove behind him. The limbs clatter in the wind, camouflaging its stalkers.

Polk walks on the sides of his feet to dampen the sound, but his commotion still echoes about. He moves to the edge, looks down at the vast fields below. Then he sees it: glowing prints. The paint. Whether it is the foggy haze, moonlight, and sunrise occupying the same world, or perhaps his own split eyelid distorting things, or if it is perhaps God himself, he does not know. But those painted tracks glow. All those tertiary colors erupting from the ground. Colors that do not belong to this season or to this place.

Polk sits on the edge, his feet dangling. He stares at the painted prints. It is the prettiest thing he has ever seen, he cannot look away, like staring into the belly of a fire. New colors. He loses track of time, just stares, his breaths coming quicker. They seem alive, crawling tracks, blurry emissions from the core of the earth.

"Is this what you wanted me to see?" he says aloud, his voice bleating through the hush. He waits for a response he knows is not coming. After all this? Mrs. Roudebush was wrong.

Polk hears the soft padding of paws before he sees the dog. A thin squeaking sound, fresh snow being tamped down. Not so much a palpable noise as an echo with no architect. He is afraid to turn around, to see what he already knows is there. When he does turn, he first notices the ribcage bulging through skin and fur. Such hunger. That distinctive brindle pattern, writhing, uncoiling around the torso. The low rumbling of anger, not a simple growl but slow-burning fury surfacing. Behind it, more movement in the cottonwood grove, a slow swaying not caused by wind. Polk stands slowly, his heels hanging over the edge of the roofline, afraid to make any quick movements. Is this about survival? Or is it revenge? The pit bull encroaches like a lurching shadow, deliberate and menacing steps, its muscled haunches tightly drawn and trembling. Polk edges along the roofline, but there is no retreat, no escape.

He turns away, looks back down at the glowing prints. He can see very far, miles, can see the individual glass panes of windows in the skyscrapers downtown and the mossy roofs of hundreds of houses on the East Side. All the city is out there, yawning itself awake. He looks down. Is it far enough to kill him? Or just to maim? To break his body apart. He pictures this for a moment, tries to feel the swelling terror in his gut as he plummets, the piercing ripple shooting through his legs, collapsing his body into an accordion when he strikes ground. Would this be the moment of relief? He wonders when the pain would strike, how long after impact? One second? Five? Never? He wonders about the precise instant when life stops and death starts. He wonders about that moment for his mother, for all the dogs he has killed.

The low rumbling draws closer, so close it seems to emanate from Polk himself. He squats down, his back to the pit bull, cinching his body into a defensive crouch. He squeezes, fights against trembling. And yet some strange joy tempers the fear, like a return to the world. He closes his good eye and waits, several ragged breaths he waits.

When he opens his eye again he sees in the distance the baseball field, the chain-link fence of its backstop. That small scoop of sledding hill next to it, so much smaller than he remembers. There it is, no so far away, a handful of blocks to the west. Has it been there this whole time? His mother pushing him down, his father dragging him back up. And then he is falling, skittering downward, spinning in some wobbly oblong orbit, the pull of gravity on his stomach. He will crash, he can feel it, he is moving too fast, out of control. Once unleashed, gravity takes over, no stopping it. Blood pulses into his head and he clamps his eyes shut and multicolored stars pour over him like a meteor shower. A piercing throb. His breath catches and he clenches, hardening muscle into concrete, bracing for impact, and when it comes, it jars the breath loose from him, and all seems lost until his father pulls him up and brushes the snow from his face and says, *Should we go again?*

Acknowledgments

"Queen Elizabeth" was originally published in *One Story* 218. Also, this story is forthcoming in Laura Furman, ed., *The O. Henry Prize Stories 2018* (New York: Anchor Books, 2018).

"Throwing Leather" was originally published in *Ascent* (September 2010).

"Evolution of the Mule" was originally published in *Beloit Fiction Journal* 25. Also, this story was anthologized in Joe Taylor, ed., *Tartts Seven: Incisive Fiction from Emerging Writers* (Livingston, AL: Livingston Press, 2016).

"The Era of Good Feelings" was originally published in *Midwestern Gothic* 20.

"How to Throw a Punch" was originally published in *The Adroit Journal* 6.

"Unicorn Stew" was originally published in *The Minnesota Review* 78.

"Stones We Throw" was originally published in *Wilderness House Literary Review* 8, no. 4.

"In the Walls" was originally published in *Atticus Review* 2, no. 34.

"Out of the Bronx" was originally published in *Zone 3* 20, no. 1.

"Hide-and-Seek" was originally published in *Sequestrum* (Spring 2015).

"Country Lepers" was originally published in *The Summerset Review* 41.

"Praemonitus, Praemunitus" was originally published in *Ostrich Review* 4.

"Patriots" was originally published in *Harpur Palate* 14, no. 2.

"The Dogs of Detroit" was originally published in *Colorado Review* 41, no. 2.

Writing and publishing a book is such a collaborative effort, though it always seems that the author gets all the credit. I've had hundreds of people guide me over the years, and while I can't thank all of them here, I would like to offer a few words of thanks.

To my mother for reading to me as a child, for showing me the value of hard work, for pushing me to be a person of *substance* in a world so infatuated with *flash*. And to my father for encouraging me to write stories long before I had any business doing so.

To Drue Heinz for her many years of supporting the literary arts. You left behind such a profound legacy. And to Lynne Sharon Schwartz for selecting this manuscript. It's surreal to see my name anywhere near yours.

To Katie Grimm, my super-agent and partner and friend. I'm so grateful that we're doing this together.

To Karen Heath for her distinctive blend of intellect and grace. You always took my writing seriously, which convinced me to take myself more seriously too.

To Hannah Tinti for all her guidance and encouragement. You give so much of yourself to help other writers that it's a wonder you have anything left for your own brilliant stories.

To Anne Valente for her innate generosity, and also for always being the best writer in the room even while being so quiet about it.

To Lawrence Coates and Wendell Mayo for years of advice, encouragement, and friendship.

To all the editors who shepherded these stories in their early forms, particularly Steven Schwartz, Chris Fink, and Barry Kitterman.

To Paul Harding, Stratis Haviaras, and Greg Harris—wonderful teachers, and you influenced my writing far more than you probably know.

To Danielle Burkin for her incredible fortitude and her proficiency in all things, which keeps me sane most days. But mostly for your friendship, which I cherish.

To Peter Kracht, Maria Sticco, Alex Wolfe, Chloe Wertz, and the entire team at the University of Pittsburgh Press. That I get to hold this book in my hands is such a marvel, and I'm so grateful that you made it happen.

To all my students over the years—thank you for your enthusiasm, which is utterly infectious.

To Henry and Graham for being the best possible distractions from writing. Being your daddy is my favorite thing in the world.

And, of course, to Susie. Without you, there's no way this book would exist, but without you, I also wouldn't even care if it did. Love you madly.